IRAN

IRAN

Open Hearts in a Closed Land

Mark Bradley

Authentic

MILTON KEYNES ● COLORADO SPRINGS ● HYDERABAD

Copyright © 2007 Mark Bradley

13 12 11 10 09 08 07   7 6 5 4 3 2 1

First published 2007 by Authentic Media
9 Holdom Avenue, Bletchley, Milton Keynes, Bucks, MK1 1QR, UK
1820 Jet Stream Drive, Colorado Springs, CO 80921, USA
OM Authentic Media, Medchal Road, Jeedimetla Village,
Secunderabad 500 055, A.P., India
www.authenticmedia.co.uk
Authentic Media is a division of IBS-STL U.K., limited by
guarantee, with its Registered Office at Kingstown Broadway,
Carlisle, Cumbria CA3 0HA. Registered in England & Wales No.
1216232. Registered charity 270162

British Library Cataloguing in Publication Data

A catalogue record for this book is available from the
British Library

ISBN-13: 978-1-85078-770-9

*Some of the names in this book have been changed to protect
identities.

Cover Design by David Smart
Print Management by Adare Carwin
Printed in Great Britain by J.H. Haynes & Co., Sparkford

Contents

Acknowledgements   vii
Foreword   ix
Introduction   xv

1. **A CLOSED LAND**   1
   The glory of Islam
   The return of Mahdi
   Anger at "Christian" West
   Impact on the church

2. **OPEN HEARTS**   44
   Disillusionment with Islamic government
   Non-Islamic identity
   Witness of the church
   The future

   Conclusion   101
   Endnotes   105
   Further Reading   115

ACKNOWLEDGEMENTS

I would like to thank Eagle Eye for giving me the opportunity to write this short book, reading the manuscript and, true to his name, saving me from some embarrassing errors.

MB, 2007

FOREWORD

by David Aray

I was about to speak at a Wednesday evening church service about Iran, the country of my birth. It was a perfect spring evening in Corpus Christi, Texas and I reasoned that there would not be many people here with a positive view of Iran. So I was excited to share with them that in spite of all the negative news reports, God is powerfully at work in Iran and building his church.

In line with much of the local population, there were a significant number of rather well-to-do retired people present. As I was speaking with a few of them before the service, one elderly lady came up to me and announced, "The best three weeks of my life were spent in Iran in 1973."

At first I thought she must have been just trying to be pleasant, but I noticed there was not even a hint of exaggeration in her voice. She went on, "You see, my son lived and worked in Iran in the early 1970s and we went out in 1973 to be with him for a short time. I just loved the people, the places, the food, the culture, the history . . . it was all just perfect. It really was the most enjoyable three weeks of my life."

I was both taken aback and happy at the same time. Here was an American lady who had lived for over eighty years in the most prosperous nation on earth, and the best three weeks of her life were spent in Iran! What a compliment.

So, not everyone has a negative view of Iran after all. Well, not everyone who can remember Iran before its 1979 Islamic revolution. Those whose memories stretch back that far, recall that Iran was a great friend to America and the West. It was, as our friend in Corpus Christi experienced, a popular tourist desti- nation and a great place to work and live. On the other hand, many people who cannot remember Iran before 1979 often think of the country only as an enemy. What else, they reason, is a nation that chants death threats to America and opposes the Western way of life?

What happened? Why does it matter to you and me as Christians? *Open Hearts in a Closed Land* will answer these questions for you. It is a very well writ- ten, accurate and clear account of the recent history of Iran. Once you have read it, the news coming out of the region will certainly make more sense to you. But this book will do more that just educate you; it will give you hope and courage for the advancement of the gospel.

Most Christians in the West are frightened of the news coming out of the Middle East. They are very fearful when they think about the Islamic world. They do not understand it and they are unable to see how the hand of God is at work in the midst of the turmoil. By looking at the history behind Iran's Islamic revolution and the resulting spiritual impact, this book describes not a bleak picture for Christianity, but rather one of great opportunity for the global church.

My family has been privileged to see this missions' opportunity develop over the last several decades. My grandfather started prayer meetings in his home in Iran during the 1950s. He led a service in his home every day for several years and earnest prayer was offered on behalf of Iran. Although there was freedom in the country at that time, there were just a handful of Iranian Muslims who had become Christians.

I know others who have worked with the Iranian church for many years. I remember in the early 1980s, when there was still little church growth, how they would get on the phone to celebrate the news of just one Iranian who had accepted Christ and recruit prayer for the new believer. Each new Iranian

Christian was a milestone, a cause for much rejoicing.

As time has passed, the frequency of such telephone calls increased and Iranians seemed to be more responsive to Jesus. People began to speak of disillusionment in Iran. Tens of thousands were fleeing the country and many Iranians were showing the signs of looking for alternative answers in life. Despite the threat of persecution, more were becoming Christians. As you read this book, you will learn why these changes began to take place and why Iranians have now become the most open Muslim people to the gospel.

In 1979, there were probably less than a thousand Iranian Christians from a Muslim background. Today, there are hundreds of house churches and while it is impossible to tell how many people have accepted Jesus, there are certainly many thousands.

Whereas my grandfather lived in a time of a handful of converts, I now seek to serve the church in Iran at a time when we could be on the brink of what could be a very significant move of the Holy Spirit. God is causing his church to grow, and I believe the church in Iran will play a significant role in taking the love of Christ to other parts of the Muslim world.

I trust that as you read *Open Hearts in a Closed Land*, you will see why I believe this. I also pray that as you learn about Iran you will be open to playing your own role, whatever it may be, in seeing the church grow in this great nation.

David Aray
USA

David Aray has been involved in serving the Iranian Church all his adult life.

INTRODUCTION

Veiled in black, the women chant "Death to America! Death to Israel!"; thousands of young men volunteer to become suicide bombers; vigilante groups on motorcycles prowl the streets looking for any clothes, make-up or amusements that would betray the glory of Islam.

Welcome to Iran.

For Western politicians, Iran is a dangerous part of George Bush's "axis of evil"; a country that has long been spitting at America, and now seems determined to develop nuclear power. In Washington, the agenda is containment, sanctions, or regime change.

But for Christians, Iran is a country of 67 million people who need to hear about the salvation of Jesus Christ. The agenda is mission, however hostile the temporal powers.

The Iranian government is certainly hostile to the Christian gospel. Evangelism, the printing of Scriptures, home Bible studies – all are illegal. And overshadowing any spiritual work is the law of apostasy that demands the execution for any Iranian born a Muslim who changes their religion. Harassment, imprisonment and even death threaten the active church member. So far, eight Christian leaders have paid the ultimate price. Behind this legislation and policy of intimidation lies a mentality that despises Christianity. There is disdain for the supposed inferiority of Jesus' teaching to the prophet of Islam's, there is scorn for the sensuous and consumerist society Christianity has spawned, and there is contempt for the attempts by any Western leader who proposes that Muslim Iran has anything to learn from the Christian West.

And yet, despite this contempt, despite the constant threats faced by Christians, despite the apostasy law, despite the strict anti-Christian legislation in place – more Iranian Muslims have become Christian in the last twenty-five years than at any other time in the history of the country since the coming of Islam to Iran in the mid seventh century.

This turning of people to Christ has got nothing to do with slick, sophisticated, expensive missionary activity, as the international church has hardly given any resources to reach Iran. No – it is not about programs, it is about people. It is that the hearts of ordinary Iranians are open to hearing about Jesus Christ. And when they hear and understand, they often believe, despite the price they have to pay.

Iran is, then, a country of *Open Hearts in a Closed Land* and the aim of this short book is to explain why this is so in the hope that it will encourage more Christians to support mission to Iran. For, as many studies have shown, effective mission is about reaching people when they are responsive. In our generation Iranians have become very responsive and if millions more of them heard the gospel of Jesus Christ, and hundreds of thousands responded – this would change the character of the Middle East.

1.

A CLOSED LAND

The ayatollahs, not the people

In some parts of the Muslim world, it is the people on the street who make it virtually impossible for Christians to be active. This is the situation in the North West Frontier Province of Pakistan. Here the actual constitution of the state allows for the free propagation of religion, but the fierce Islamic fundamentalism of the Pathan people makes Christian mission very dangerous.

In Iran it is the opposite. The majority of the people in Iran are not fierce fundamentalist fanatics. From a population of 67 million, only 28 million people actually voted in the second round of the 2005 elections and, of these, only 17 million voted for the hardline fundamentalist president Ahmadinejad. And, as stated by some reporters, many voted for him either because of peer pressure, or because he promised to put Iran's oil money on their dining room tables.[1]

This means that it is very likely that less than 25 per cent of the population is fundamentalist. It could be a lot less.

However, it is this minority which supports the ayatollahs who control all the machinery of the national and local government, and they own all the guns. This makes them an all-powerful force, and allows them to close Iran to the gospel. It is the opposition of these ayatollahs we first want to look into. We will see that their hostility is rooted in their belief in the glory of Islam, faith in the return of Mahdi and an intense suspicion of the West. We will also see that this hostility does not flow out of the mists of time or primarily out of religious textbooks – rather, it is a hostility which springs from very recent Iranian history.

Hostility Factor 1: The glory of Islam

Shortly after coming to power in the 2005 elections, President Ahmadinejad called together all the leaders of Non-Governmental Organizations (NGOs) in Tehran for a meeting. He told them that the Iranian government supported all their good work, but they must not forget one thing. The NGOs must make sure that all their activities were for the glory of Islam.

The glory of Islam – this is the rationale behind controlling people's dress codes, stopping mixed-sex swimming, not allowing women to attend soccer matches, censoring music, banning card games, and the government's treatment of Christianity. This indeed is the raison d'etre of the 1979 revolution that fundamentally changed the way all Muslim states thought about the relationship between religion and the government.

Reaction to royalist attack on Islam

And it was a major change. Before the 1979 revolution, the devout were concerned with the glory of Islam, but there was never any suggestion that the Muslim leaders should control all the levers of power in the state. Instead it was accepted that the religious leaders would have influence on the state, rather like in Medieval Christendom when bishops would have a quiet word in the ears of the kings.[2]

The idea that Muslim leaders should actually rule the country was unheard of. Indeed, it was almost blasphemous in Iran, which is 89 per cent Shi'a. This is because the Shi'as believe that the only perfect government will occur when the Twelfth Imam returns. For any Muslim to think he – it would certainly be a he – could rule in the place of this Twefth Imam was excessive presumption.[3]

But this is exactly what the 1979 revolution ushered in – the rule of the ayatollahs. What had happened to bring about such a fundamental shift in Iran's political thinking?

The answer is Ayatollah Khomeini and his reaction to the Pahlavi kings who attacked Islam and courted the Christian West. Abrupt and dictatorial, Reza Shah, who reigned from 1925–41, was a soldier-king, always in uniform, always wanting to get things done. Inspired by Kemal Ataturk of Turkey, he was determined to modernize Iran. And for that to happen, technology had to increase, and religion had to decrease.

And so Reza Shah built roads, railways, and factories, schools, colleges: and he attacked religion. He took education away from the mullahs, abolished religious courts, made it illegal for women to wear the veil, and forced all working men to wear a special cap, known as the "Pahlavi" cap.

All protest was suppressed. On hearing that one Sayyid Ghazanfaar was claiming to be the Twelfth Imam, Reza Shah ordered the man's arrest, famously saying: "During my reign I will not permit any prophets to appear."[4] Sometimes he was more brutal. Once there was an outcry in Mashed, Iran's holiest city, about these "Pahlavi" caps. The mullahs said that when men prayed, their foreheads could not touch the ground, as they were meant to. Reza Shah's answer was to send in his soldiers who shot and killed one hundred protesters.[5]

Khomeini's revolutionary theory of Valayat-e Faqih

Watching all this with horror was the young Ayatollah Ruhollah Khomeini. From a well-connected landowning clerical family, his writings and lectures had made him one of Qom's most famous religious teachers by the 1950s. In the early 1960s he became a political force.

It was in the context of Islam being attacked by a powerful secular ruler that Ayatollah Khomeini developed a radical new Islamic political doctrine. At its heart was the concept of the *Valayat-e Faqih* which literally translates as the rule of the jurisprudent. To counter the rule of corrupt kings who sneered at Islam and courted unclean foreign powers, Khomeini's vision was for an Islamic Republic ruled by a supreme spiritual leader. Just as Reza Shah completely rejected any role for religion in his new technological Iran, so now Khomeini rejected any role for secular politicians in a pure Islamic state. The theological argument was simple: Islam was a complete system of law and morality, and therefore only the most learned in Islam could govern properly.

Also behind the theology was a very practical argument. The Pahlavis had shown that secular rulers could not be trusted to preserve Islam: they had marginalized Islam and promoted a quasi national religion based on the glory of Iran's ancient kings. For Khomeini the choice facing the Iranian nation was stark – monarchy or the glory of Islam.

It was this choice that Khomeini put relentlessly to the Iranian people in the 1970s. He constantly branded the Shah as a pathetic poodle of the US who was humiliating Iran and Islam with his obsession with Western fashion, which he termed "Westoxication". Through cassette tapes and radio broadcasts from exile, first in Iraq and then in Paris, he called on Iranians to reject their puppet king and return to their national and religious roots symbolized in Shi'a Islam.[6]

On February 1 1979, Ayatollah Khomeini, forty-seven of his closest male followers, and 141 journalists boarded a chartered Air France Boeing 747 and flew to Iran. During the journey an announcement was made that the Iranian Air Force was going to shoot down the plane, but this never happened, and after encircling Tehran airport three times the plane landed and Khomeini stepped out to be welcomed by millions.

It seemed Iran had chosen the glory of Islam.

Thousands of the people who came out cheering for Khomeini that day had never read his writings about the *Valayat-e Faqih*. They saw this seventy-seven year-old ayatollah as the symbolic head of the resistance to rid Iran of the dictatorial Shah whose troops were shooting demonstrators in the street. Those people never dreamt that Khomeini would lead a government, not least because he always denied he wanted to. He said he just wanted to be a "guide". So the communists, the socialists, the nationalists, the liberals – all the anti-royalist groups – welcomed the arrival of the old man. He had done his job of getting rid of the Shah, now they could argue over who would actually run the country. For a while this was also the view of the American leader, President Carter. He and many others in Washington believed that Khomeini would soon realize he could not run a complex country like Iran. He would retire to teach in Qom, leaving the Western educated liberals in charge. And they would probably be a lot easier to deal with than the prickly, proud Shah with his illusions of imperial grandeur.[7]

They all underestimated Khomeini. He established himself as the *Valayat-e Faqih*, the Guardian (also known as the Supreme Spiritual Leader), appointed the government and established a constitution that made sure every aspect of policy could be controlled to implement his interpretation of the glory of Islam.

Government of Mirrors[8] leaves all power with Valayat-e Faqih

In a few months the whole apparatus of the Shah's government was swept away and replaced by institutions which have ruled Iran now for over twenty-five years. They are institutions which are both democratic and dictatorial. So when Ayatolloah Khomeini died on June 3 1989, it fell to the Council of Experts to choose his successor, the present Supreme Leader, Ayatollah Khamenei. The seventy-three members of the Council of Experts are voted in by the people, so it seems there is a democratic element in the system. However, all candidates can be vetoed by the Council of Guardians whose six members are directly chosen by the Supreme Leader. It is a mirrors system whereby the Supreme Leader seems to be elected by the people, but in reality is chosen by the faithful.

The mirrors continue when you look at the national government. It is led by an elected president who is accountable to an elected parliament which has to approve the president's cabinet. However, the Supreme Leader can veto any parliamentary candidate, as happened to 2,500 hopefuls in the 2004 elections;[9] and indeed intervene in any area of government whenever he wishes. Furthermore, no law can be passed until it has been checked by the Council of Guardians. So the elected government can be overruled at any time by the Supreme Leader.

Throughout the country there is a similar mirror system of government. There is the mayor's office and the usual departments of provincial government, and there are also the local *Komitehs* operated by the mosque and the bazaar. These are essentially vigilante groups committed to defending Khomeini's revolution. It is these *Komitehs* which will launch patrols to check on people's clothing, or raid private homes for alcohol – or report on Christian activity. The *Komitehs* are supported by the Revolutionary Tribunals which operate again a mirror judicial system alongside the official courts. These tribunals can charge people with the very broad accusation of "insulting Islam" and then both imprison, or even execute defendants.

Supporting the whole system are the Revolutionary Guards who mirror the official army. Created in May 1979 to ensure support for the new revolution, the Revolutionary Guards numbered more than a hundred thousand within a year. They receive more funds than the official military and they report directly to the Supreme Leader. If there was ever a lack of support from the official army, there are always the Revolutionary Guards.[10]

So in the space of a few months, Ayatollah Khomeini set up a government that had some of the trappings of a democratic state, but in effect handed over all power to the *Valayat-e Faqih* who would ensure society lived for the glory of Islam.

It is the glory of Islam that ensures docile Christians live as second-class citizens, while active Christians face persecution.

Christians: Existence tolerated; prosperity barred

When Islam first swept out of Arabia, many Christians and Jews came under the new religion's rule. As "people of the book" they were allowed to practise their religion, but they also had to accept they were second-class citizens. They would be tolerated, but they would never be allowed to have any significant influence. This has been exactly the case for the Assyrian (Nestorian) Christians who were very widespread when Islam first conquered Iran in the middle of the seventh century. This has also been the case for the Armenians who were brought to Iran in the early seventeenth century, to help build Shah Abbas' new capital, Isfahan. Many more Armenians fled to Iran during the Turkish genocide in the early twentieth century. Both the Assyrian and Armenian communities are tolerated by the Islamic government; but they are not allowed to have any influence in the country. Not surprisingly, thousands have left Iran since 1979.

The brave Christian

At the end of that meeting held by Ahmadinejad to urge NGOs to work for the glory of Islam, one Christian put up his hand and asked, "Mr President, I am very happy to make sure all my work helps Iran

. . . but I am a Christian. How can I work for the glory of Islam?" Ahmadinejad replied that his officials would get in touch with him later. They certainly did. A few days later the secret police arrived, took the Christian to their offices and questioned him. They advised him to make sure he left the country as soon as possible, or they could not guarantee his safety. This perfectly illustrates the way the government barely tolerates Christians. As long as they stay quiet and just exist, they are not necessarily intimidated. But as soon as Christians speak out – they get into serious trouble.

Evangelism – A double-edged sword of shame for Islam

Christians are barely tolerated – and all evangelism is completely illegal as it is a double-edged sword of shame for the glory of Islam. First of all, evangelism dishonors Islam because it undermines the belief the Koran was God's last revelation to humankind. This is indeed a part of the glory of Islam. So for a Muslim to be told that they have to repent of their sins and believe in Christ to be saved, thus implying there is not perfect and complete salvation in their religion, this insults Islam. And then secondly, if the evangelism is successful, while the church has a new convert, the Muslim community has an apostate whose very existence shames Islam. Thus the apostate must be killed.

For the genuine Muslim there is no getting away from the fact that his religion does truly call on the devout to kill apostates. The rule is in both the Koran and in the Hadiths (the traditions about Mohammad).

In the Koran there is Sura 4:89

> They would have you disbelieve as they themselves have done, so that you may all be alike. Do not befriend them until they have fled their homes for the cause of Allah. If they desert you, seize them and put them to death wherever you find them.[11]

Other verses from the Koran also quoted as supporting execution for apostates are: Sura 5:59; Sura 16:108; and Sura 2:213.

The Hadiths, the some six hundred thousand traditional sayings about the Muslim prophet, have almost equal authority among Muslims, and here also death for the apostate is recommended. So we read in An-Nawawi's collection of Hadiths.

> The Apostle of God said the blood of a fellow-Muslim should never be shed except in three cases; that of the adulterer, the murderer, and whoever forsakes the religion of Islam.[12]

And in the most famous collection of Bukhari it is bluntly stated that Mohammad said

Whosoever changes his religion, kill him[13]

It should be stressed that the vast majority of Iranians would never dream of killing an apostate. There are even many in the government who would hesitate to actually bring an apostate before a firing squad. But nevertheless there are enough Iranians in the government committed to enforcing the law of apostasy and this makes Iran very closed to Christianity. These people are motivated by the "glory of Islam".

A European was once on a domestic flight to Tehran and found himself sitting next to a friendly Iranian man who immediately began to ask many questions once he realized the European could speak some Persian. After all the questions, the European asked the Iranian what his job was, and the man proudly replied that he was a *Pasdar* in *Sepah*, which means he was a senior leader in the Revolutionary Guards.

On hearing this the European said, "Well, I have some questions for you . . . all these people on this plane were born Muslims. Say they had a vision about Jesus Christ, or they read the Gospels and sincerely believed that Christ died for their sins, so they become Christian. What do you think should happen to them?"

The reply was chilling. *"Edam* (execution)," said the *Pasdar*.

His colleague in the next seat, not wanting to give such a negative impression of Iran to a European, shook his head and said, "No, we do not execute in Iran."

But the senior man was not to be contradicted.

"Yes, we certainly do execute apostates," he said, and then he started quoting religious texts in Arabic.

"But," said the European, "why can't these people be free to choose their own religion? Why should they be killed?"

In reply, the *Pasdar* tapped the top of the seat in front of him and said: "The glory of the Koran . . . the glory of the Koran."

This story perfectly illustrates the situation in Iran. Most people would be like the *Pasdar's* friend; they are uncomfortable with the apostasy law. But the people who have power in the country, they are like the *Pasdar* who believe that apostates should be killed to ensure the glory of Islam. And it is this belief that has caused the death of at least five Christian leaders in Iran: Reverend Sayyah, who was brutally murdered in Shiraz in 1979; Reverend Soodmand, who was hanged in Mashad prison in 1990; Mehdi Dibaj, who was sentenced to death for apostasy by an Islamic court in 1993, was then released after an international outcry, only to be later murdered in Tehran in the summer of

1994; 'Ravanbaksh', who was found hung in the north of Iran in September 1996; and Ghorbandordi Tourani who was stabbed to death in front of his wife in November 2005.

Persian – a very dangerous language for evangelism

The situation is exacerbated by the fact that the historic Christians in Iran, the Assyrians and Armenians, speak a different language with different alphabets to the Iranians. So whereas in Arabic countries the churches can print material in Arabic because this is the language of the historic Christians, and tell the Muslim authorities it is just for the Christians, in Iran this is not possible. If the Christians print any material in Persian then it means it is immediately for Muslims – because there are no historic Persian-speaking Christians in Iran. The Iranian government is very strict about this, because evangelistic material undermines the glory of Islam.

A government official was once approached by a printer who wanted to publish Christian material in Persian. The printer was hoping to then get some good orders, but the government official brought an end to this plan. He said that Christian material could only be printed in Assyrian or Armenian, and then added in an unnerving tone that any publisher who printed Christian material in Persian would deserve execution.

The glory of Islam closes Iran

As soon as Ayatollah Khomeini arrived to the cheers of millions in February 1979, Iran became a closed land to the gospel. For the whole raison d'etre of the government he established is the glory of Islam. Christians existing as a dying weak breed can be tolerated, but all Christian evangelism must be stopped for it insults the heart of Iran's government – the glory of Islam.

Hostility Factor 2: **The return of Mahdi**

President Ahmadinejad's debut on the world stage at the United Nations on September 17 2005 caused quite a stir. For after bluntly stating that human beings are only happy when they follow monotheism (i.e. Islam), attacking US foreign policy, and robustly defending Iran's rights to nuclear power, Ahmadinejad then ended his speech with a prayer.

> Oh Lord hasten the emergence of your last repository, the Promised One, that perfect and pure human being, the one that will fill this world with justice and peace.[14]

Who is this "Promised One"? Who is this "perfect and pure human being" who brings justice and peace? The answer is Mahdi, the Twelfth Imam, who disappeared mysteriously as a young boy of five in the ninth century. The main difference between the Sunnis and the Shi'as is that the Shi'as believe that the leaders of the Muslim community have to be from Mohammad's family. These are known as Imams. Ali, Mohammad's son-in-law was the First Imam, and Mahdi was the Twelfth. When he went missing, there could be no more Imams – because though he cannot be seen, Mahdi is still around. He is in hiding, and at the end of the world he will come back (with Jesus in the back seat), to restore the world to justice.[15]

The Revolutionary Government has always stressed the importance of Mahdi, but Ahmadinejad has taken public devotion to new levels. There have been reports that when he was mayor of Tehran he secretly instructed the city council to build an avenue to prepare for Mahdi's return, and an early act of his cabinet was to earmark $17 million to rebuild the Jamkaran Mosque just outside Qom. It is widely believed Mahdi will answer prayers if written requests are dropped down a well very near to this mosque. There are also plans to build a direct train link between Tehran and Jamkaran so pilgrims can visit the site more easily. There have even been rumors that Ahmadinejad's entire cabinet has signed a letter to Mahdi which has also been sent down the Jamkaran well.[16]

In public, Ahmadinejad has repeatedly stated that this is the aim of his government: to bring back Mahdi.[17] Soon after taking office, he led the Friday prayers at Tehran University, which is the normal platform for outlining government policy and this is what he said

> Our revolution's main mission is to pave the way for the reappearance of the 12th Imam, the Mahdi, so today, we should define our economic, cultural and political policies based on the policy of Imam Mahdi's return[18]

And in nearly all his speeches, President Ahmadinejad returns to this theme. Some supporters have even suggested that he is one of the specially chosen by Mahdi in each generation to be an *Owtad*, a "nail". According to Shi'a traditions, the hidden Imam chooses thirty-six men to be "nails" who are then hammered into the human race to keep it from falling down. Ahmadinejad has never disputed these claims. In fact he is quite happy to encourage the idea that he is a specially chosen Owtad.[19]

After his debut at the United Nations, he told a friend

> I felt that all of a sudden the atmosphere changed,
> and for 27 to 28 minutes the leaders did not blink.
> They were astonished . . . it had opened their eyes
> and ears for the message of the Islamic Republic.[20]

His conclusion was that "the Hidden Imam drenched the place in a sweet light."[21]

Without a doubt, the president is sure of strengthening his support by cultivating his image of one of the hidden Imam's specially chosen ones, for Mahdi has always been very popular in Iran. He has been the symbol of hope ever since the Shi'a faith was adopted nationally by the Iranians at the beginning of the sixteenth century. So many Iranians will complain about all their problems, and then say at the end with a resigned sigh, "Well, everything will be all right when Mahdi returns." The crowd of two thousand or more in Jamkaran certainly believe in Mahdi's power. One lady there told a journalist that she had been healed by Mahdi; a banker from nearby Qom said that his prayer had been answered after coming for forty nights in a row. Now he had a new request and would come for another forty nights.[22] Similar stories would be repeated across the country.

Some observers believe that Ahmadinejad, a non-cleric leader in a country run by clerics, is cynically using Mahdi to bolster his political legitimacy. Certainly his fervour for the hidden Imam increases

his popular support, but Ahmadinejad's commitment is deeper. Shortly after his election victory, but
before appointing his cabinet, Ahmadinejad visited
Ayatollah Mohammad Taqi Mesbah-Yazdi, a radical
and extremely influential religious leader in Qom
who fervently campaigns for the return of Mahdi.
Ahmadinejad would have certainly thanked
Mesbah-Yazdi, as this ayatollah issued a fatwa urg-
ing voters to support him which proved crucial in
securing victory. He would also have taken advice,
soon seen when Ahmadinejad appointed his new
government. There was a wholesale removal of all
officials who were in any way seen as compromis-
ers or reformers to the original spirit of the Islamic
revolution, and the appointment of rigid hardliners,
a number of them alumnae from the Haghani
School where Mesbah-Yazdi has been a senior lec-
turer.[23]

Now in his seventies, Mesbah-Yazdi has been con-
sidered extreme, even by the hardliner founders of the
regime, Khomeini, Rafsanjani and Khamenei. Mesbah-
Yazdi rejects all pluralism, every way of life and every
thought that does not match up to a strict literal interpretation of Shi'a Islam. He certainly rejects all other
religions apart from Islam, so Christianity and
Judaism are completely unclean, but he also vehemently opposes all deviations from the Shi'a faith,
within Islam. So he is hostile to long-established

heretics, the Baha'is and the Sunnis, and it is widely rumored he is a member of the semi-secret Hojattieh group. This group fervently campaigns for the return of Mahdi, and actively works against all heretics. Mesbah-Yazdi constantly denounced the last president Mohammad Khatami for giving some freedom to intellectuals. In his pronouncements, Mesbah-Yazdi likened these intellectuals to Satan, who dared to question the authority of God. For this they "Deserve to be treated the way we should treat Satan . . . O! Death with such wayward human beings!"[24]

Mesbah-Yazdi often advocates death for his opponents; indeed Mohammad Khatami has publicly called him the "theoretician of violence."[25] Mesbah-Yazdi has said that those who want to reform Islam should be hit in the face: "If someone tells you he has a new interpretation of Islam, sock him in the mouth."[26] Those who offend Islam should just be instantly killed without any legal procedures: "If anyone insults the Islamic sanctities, Islam has permitted for his blood to be spilled, no court needed either."[27] One of the ayatollah's heroes, whom he regularly praises, is Nawab Safavi, the founder of Fadaiyan Islam, which murdered many supposedly un-Islamic Iranian politicians and intellectuals in the mid-twentieth century. By supporting Nawab Safavi, Mesbah-Yazdi is giving his blessing to the assassins who murdered many intellectuals and journalists in 1998 for allegedly insulting Islam.

Mesbah-Yazdi is just as keen on violence when it comes to foreign affairs. In the past, other senior Muslim clerics have stated that both suicide bombing and nuclear weapons are against the tenets of Islam. Mesbah-Yazdi is a supporter of both. On his website he argues vigorously for the Palestinians to use suicide bombers in their campaign to uproot the "arrogant" Israelis. So we read on the ayatollah's website:[28] "When protecting Islam, the Muslim Ummah depends on martyrdom operations, it is not only allowed, but even it is an obligation (*wajib*)." He is also a driving force behind Iran's "Lovers Of Martyrdom Garrison" and advertisements for recruits have appeared in the newspaper *Parto-Sokhan*. This is published by the Imam Khomeini Education and Research Institute, of which Mesbah-Yazdi is the director.

To the international world, Iran's leadership has always maintained that it only wants to develop nuclear power for energy purposes. Indeed, the Supreme Leader, Ayatollah Khamenei, has declared that it is against Islam for a Muslim nation to hold nuclear weapons. This has now been contradicted by Mohsen Gharavian, a spokesman for Mesbah-Yazdi who in February 2006 said

For the first time the use of nuclear weapons may not constitute a problem, according to Sharia . . . When the entire world is armed with nuclear weapons, it is permissible to use these weapons as a counter-measure. According to Sharia too, only the goal is important.[29]

All of this violence is justified in Mesbah-Yazdi's mind because he is a fervent believer in the return of Mahdi. As a Shi'a leader he has a duty to prepare not just Iran, but the whole world for this eschatological event. On his website he writes

We are expected to do our best in actualizing Islamic rulings in our personal as well as social life, and to establish the Just Islamic System all over the world in order to pave the way for the reappearance of Baqiyat-Allah al-a'dham (may our souls be consecrated for him, and may Allah hasten his auspicious return.)

If killing heretics and infidels, who will burn in hell anyway, helps establish this Islamic system and so hastens the return of the one who will restore peace and justice, then the use of violence is perfectly logical.

It is this ayatollah who is the spiritual mentor of Iran's president which is why Ahmadinejad's references to the return of Mahdi are not superficial. And

there is no reason to believe that this alliance between
Mesbah-Yazdi and Ahmadinejad is going to weaken.
In fact, Mesbah-Yazdi is clearly seeking to strengthen
his position in the all-important Council of Experts
which supervises and ultimately appoints the
Supreme Leader. When Ayatollah Khamenei retires,
and there have been questions about his health, it is
not wholly unlikely that Mesbah-Yazdi will try to be
Iran's next all-powerful ruler.

The power of Ahmadinejad and Mesbah-Yazdi
casts a long shadow over those wishing for more freedom within Iran and a calmer atmosphere internationally. Again, motivated by thinking they can bring
back Mahdi, they are both strict hardliners regarding
domestic freedoms, and Mesbah-Yazdi has made it
clear that democracy and Islam are not compatible

> Democracy means if the people want something that
> is against God's will, then they should forget about
> God and religion. Be careful not to be deceived.
> Accepting Islam is not compatible with democracy.[30]

Internationally, their belief in the return of Mahdi
means they are actually expecting worldwide catas-
trophes and turmoil as this will signify the Imam's
imminent return. This has certainly made President
Ahmadinejad's approach to foreign policy more con-
frontational, for if you sincerely believe that a Muslim

prophet will ultimately rule the world, why should you pretend to be entering into a dialogue with other civilizations? This is what the political editor of *Resalat* observed

> This kind of mentality makes you very strong. If I think the Mahdi will come in two, three, or four years, why should I be soft? Now is the time to stand strong, to be hard.[31]

Darker shadow for Christians

The rise of Ahmadinejad and Mesbah-Yazdi and their aim to create an Iran fit for Mahdi casts a dark and dangerous shadow over all Christians. For this whole eschatological belief system adds an extra urgency for the government to ensure that at least Iran, the only Shi'a nation in the world, is pure and undefiled. It means that apostates will absolutely not be tolerated: for not only do they insult the glory of Islam, but they delay the return of Mahdi. So it gives the fundamentalist security agencies even more religious justification to intimidate and threaten.

And it also means that there is even less concern for the government to be considerate to the historical Assyrian and Armenian communities. The story about the Christian who was taken for questioning simply for daring to say that his Christian NGO could not work for the glory of Islam clearly shows that the present government has no interest in even pretending to be inclusive. Under Mohammad Khatami, and his concern for there to be a dialogue of civilizations, there was more respect in the tone of the authorities. But the tone of the new government is clear: this country is only for Muslims. And the sub-heading to that is – we are happier if you leave.

The city of Mashad with the dazzling and vast shrine to Imam Reza, has always been fanatically Shi'a. In the 1980s, Revd Soodmand led a small group of Christians who used to meet in the basement of his home. In 1990, Revd Soodmand was found guilty of insulting Islam and hanged in the city's prison. His body was buried in a part of the cemetery reserved for the cursed. A few years later, the authorities arrested another active church member, Mohammad, and put him in prison. While there, Mohammad saw his name on a list of people likely to be executed. Mohammad passionately protested to the official, at one point saying, "You cannot kill us just because we are Christians!"

The reply was very revealing.

"Yes we can. We can clean up the whole country."

In this official's mind the question was not of justice, but of cleanliness. A defiled Iran will keep away Mahdi.

The government wants to keep Iran as a completely closed country to Christianity. They are motivated by their understanding of the glory of Islam and the desire to bring back Mahdi. These are the religious reasons, but there is also a third reason that pulsates at the heart of the Iranian government. This is the fear and hatred they have for the West and, as they see Christianity as a Western religion, this further motivates them to making sure Iran is closed to the gospel.

Hostility Factor 3: **Anger at "Christian" West**

Iranians are one of the most hospitable and polite people in the world. They genuinely and sincerely enjoy being with foreigners, and go to great lengths to ensure guests are honored. This certainly includes Westerners. Indeed Iranians have a great respect for Westerners – they admire the Europeans for their culture, and they instinctively warm to the Americans for their pioneering spirit, passion for freedom and anti-colonialism. At a personal level, there is absolutely no malice towards Westerners.

However, if the conversation turns to recent politics, the Westerner can find there is anger towards the policies of their governments, even with the friendliest of Iranians. At the heart of this anger is the fixed belief that the West has interfered with Iran to exploit her oil reserves. There is also the general Muslim anger against the West about the oppression of the Muslim Palestinians by the Israeli state, a Western creation.

Historical facts support the Iranian complaint that the West interfered with Iran politically for oil profits. The Englishman William D'Arcy purchased rights from the Iranian government to search for oil in 1901. The black gold was discovered in 1908 and the new Anglo-Iranian Oil Company invested £22 million in drilling operations. Over the next forty years they got back £800 million, while the Iranian government was just given over £100 million. Profits for Western shareholders were very good.[32]

However, the Iranians felt cheated. This was a smoldering issue in the 1930s, which then got lost in the catastrophic experience of the Second World War. The first Pahlavi king, Reza Shah, was deposed by the British for being too friendly with the Nazis, Iran was invaded, and the Shah's young son, fresh from an exclusive private school in Switzerland, was installed as king. Iran emerged from the war deeply humiliated and virtually bankrupt. Into this situation strode the aristocratic Dr Mohammad Mossadeq, who was elected as prime minister in 1951. He swept up all the country's rage and focused it on the hated English who were stealing the nation's oil. The new young Shah, installed by the English, was completely outshone and became a nervous observer as the wily old Mossadeq successfully nationalized the country's oil and drove the English from Iran's shores.

Iranians adored Mossadeq. In the tradition of all Iran's great kings, he had challenged the greed of the foreigner and put on a colorful show for his own people. They loved his flamboyance and oratory. Sometimes in the parliament he would speak constantly for two days, and then collapse in a faint. He would be taken home on a stretcher where he would hold court resting on piles of pillows, lying on his simple iron bed and dressed in pajamas. Foreigners who had to visit him in his bedroom were completely confused: Iranians loved the drama.

The British government did not. They had over a 50 per cent stake in the Anglo-Iranian Oil Company and the Persian fields were supplying nearly a quarter of the world's markets. To win them back, the British went to Washington and managed to persuade Dwight Eisenhower that Mossadeq was in fact a closet communist and Iran could fall to the Soviets. In the black and white world of the cold war, Eisenhower was not ready to see this happen and he authorized Operation Ajax which saw the CIA spend just a million dollars to oust Mossadeq.[33]

While the CIA rented crowds and used right-wing contacts in the army to encircle Mossadeq, the king, Mohammad Reza Shah, had run away to Italy where he stayed at the Excelsior Hotel. On August 20 1953, he received a telegram saying "Mossadeq over-thrown; imperial troops control Tehran." Apparently he went pale and whispered, "I knew that they loved me."[34] This of course was pure sentimentalism. Like everyone else, he knew that his power rested not on the love of the people, but on the support of the West, especially the USA.

In a recent speech, former President Clinton accurately described the 1953 coup as being one of the worst blunders in US Middle Eastern policy.[35] Till then the Americans had always been viewed favorably by the Iranians. They admired the success of this young country, they respected their commitment to democracy, and they especially liked the US hostility to the British and their Empire. After nationalizing the oil and driving the English from Iran, Mossadeq immediately got into severe financial trouble, and very revealingly he instinctively turned to the Americans for help. He assumed the Americans would support all that he and many others in Iran stood for – liberalism, democracy, and anti-colonialism. So the fact that it was the Americans who ousted Mossadeq and installed and armed a king who soon became a dictator was a very bitter shock to Iranians.

The year 1953 has never been forgotten or forgiven. Iranians now assume that all American foreign policy is designed to simply help the US economy. For

Mohammad Reza Shah proved a very faithful collaborator with America. In 1954, the Western oil companies were back at the negotiating table: the Anglo-Iranian Oil Company (now British Petroleum) was given a 40 per cent stake, and received full compensation for losses suffered during the Mossadeq period.[36] And though Iran's share rose (to 50 per cent) so there were substantial oil profits, these were all spent on American weapons. Iran under Mohammad Reza Shah developed the Middle East's most powerful military force. This force was not just to defend Iran; it was for the West's security: America and Britain wanted to use Iran as their policeman in the Middle East. The Shah also spent a lot of money on US internal security training and equipment, so soon his secret service, SAVAK, was the most feared in the region.[37]

It was this dictatorship that the present leaders of the Iranian government experienced. As they challenged the Shah and the government for being against Islam, so they found themselves being arrested by SAVAK. Ayatollah Khomeini was arrested and imprisoned for ten months before being sent into exile; Hashemi Rafsanjani was imprisoned five times and the present Supreme Leader, Ayatollah Khamenei was imprisoned six times by SAVAK where he was kept in solitary confinement and tortured. A fellow inmate described conditions at one of the Savak prisons.

> I was in cell number 18, Sayyid Khamenei in cell 20
> . . . you used to hear the moaning and cries of the
> inmates almost around the clock. The experience was
> a living example of the Qur'anic verse "They are nei-
> ther dead nor alive." The wretched inmates were
> beaten unconscious, then revived and hospitalised
> just to restore a semblance of their health so that they
> could be returned to the same routine of torture,
> using all kinds of tools and ways.[38]

Given the experience the leaders of the revolution
have had under a regime established and financed by
the USA, it is not at all surprising that they are angry,
and opposed to Christianity, the dominant religion in
America.

As well as the oppression suffered under the Shah,
the Islamic leaders were appalled at the invasion of
Western culture during his rule, and the arrogant
assumption by some that this culture was superior to
Iran's. They railed against the Shah for trying to ape
the fashions of the West, and denounced the corrupt-
ing aspects of American culture – the rock music,
miniskirts, alcohol and drugs. Ayatollah Khomeini
had cleverly called this "Westoxication",[39] and with
one word reminded all Iranians of their true cultural
roots. For Iran's most famous and popular poet,
Hafiz, constantly referred to the need for people to be
"God intoxicated". The call of Khomeini and the

country's history was for Iranians to be drunk with God, not the West. And especially not "West intoxicated" when Hollywood in the 1970s was abandoning conservative moral standards, and her stars were living increasingly hedonistic lives. Of course, Christian leaders protested against this public slide into immorality, but people in the Middle East still assumed the West was Christian. This gave their religious leaders even more reason to oppose Christianity. For not only was this religion theologically flawed, but it had produced a society obsessed with sex and materialism, soaring divorce rates, thousands of legal abortions and increasing drug and alcohol abuse.

The West's exploitation of Iran's oil, their support for the Shah and SAVAK, their sordid cultural values – these all made Iran's religious leaders angry. And then there is Israel, a constant reminder of the West's arrogant imperialism which carved up countries in the Muslim Middle East with no consultation with the people. Right from the start, the Iranian Revolutionaries were vehemently opposed to the state of Israel, and called for it to be eliminated. Ayatollah Khomeini said, "Israel must be eradicated from the page of history" and constantly called on all Muslims to help remove "This degenerative tumour that has, with the backing of major powers, been planted in the heart of Islamic states and whose roots daily threaten the Islamic lands."[40] So there is nothing new about President Ahmadinejad's tone when he says "Israel must be wiped off the map."[41]

There are four elements to Iran's hostility to Israel. First of all, they believe Jerusalem belongs to Muslims; secondly, they believe that Israel, supported by the West, drove the Muslim Palestinians illegally from their land and now oppress them; thirdly, they believe that Israel is essentially a colony of America and since it has nuclear weapons it is a dangerous threat to all Muslim countries in the Middle East; fourthly, there is a belief in some government circles that Jews are deceitful and want to dominate the whole world. President Ahmadinejad has recently been openly stating a long-held belief among revolutionary leaders that the Holocaust never happened and it is just a deceit used by the Jews to make money. Then a recent TV drama on the government-controlled Sahar 1, called *Zahra's Blue Eyes*, tells the story of an Israeli journalist who works to harvest the organs of Palestinian children. He is particularly interested in getting Zahra's blue eyes for his blind daughter. Such a program is purely anti-Semitic, seeking to show that Jews are twisted and cruel.[42] The Iranian government also publishes and publicizes a book called *The Protocols of the Elders of Zion* which is full of allegations on how the Jews want to take over the world.[43] The net effect of all this is to support the racist idea in the minds of some Iranians that there is something dangerous about the Jews. It is this anti-Semitism that gives passion to the government's constant cries for Israel to be eliminated.

Iran's hostility to Israel then is a cauldron of regional politics, religion, fear and racism. But for the Iranian leadership, the only reason why Israel is in the Middle East is because of Christian America – that is why they talk of a Christian-Zionist conspiracy.[44] So it is Christianity that is involved in supporting Iran's nearest, and most armed, enemy. This again makes the regime very closed to the gospel.

A passionate commitment to the glory of Islam; a fervent belief in the imminent return of Mahdi; and a bitter hatred for the West all pulsate along the corridors of clerical power in Iran and makes the country extremely hostile to the gospel of Jesus Christ. The idea of missionary or evangelistic work to every Iranian leader is anathema.

Iran is truly a closed country.

Impact on the church

How then does this government hostility impact Christians?

There are two main types of overground churches in Iran: the historical churches of the Assyrians and the Armenians; and the churches founded by nine-teenth-century missions, the Presbyterians and the Anglicans. The Assemblies of God Church is also an overground church, but was not founded by a foreign mission; rather it grew out of a local prayer meeting among radical Armenian Christians in the 1950s.

The policy of the government towards the Armenian and the Assyrians so far has been to offici-ally recognize them. They have representatives in par-liament (Assyrians one, Armenians two); they are allowed to print Bibles and Christian material in their own languages; they are allowed to follow their own rules regarding marriage and divorce and their church life is allowed to continue normally. This superficially gives the impression that Iran tolerates Christianity. However, the Islamic government keeps these two communities under tight control. In many of the Armenian schools, the government insists that the principal is a Muslim, and checks all the material taught. And if Armenians attend Muslim schools, then children can face the humiliation of being told that they are unclean and that the other children should wash their hands if they come into contact with the Christians. Once they leave school, the government's iron grip on the economy means that Assyrians and Armenians struggle to prosper financially and unemployment is rife. At every turn the Armenians and Assyrians hear the message that Iran is not a country for them, and conclude there is no future for their children. Consequently there has been a mass exodus to the West. If the Assyrian community had grown at the same rate as the rest of the Iranian population there should now be 1 million in Iran. In fact there are less than ten thousand. Hundreds have left the country every week. To underline how many Muslims feel about the Assyrian exodus, a local mullah in Orumieh, the town where many Assyrians live, advised his people not to buy Assyrian property, but wait till they had gone, when they could get the property for free. His comments produced outrage, but they probably exposed a widespread attitude[45]

So the policy towards these large historical churches is to tolerate, but at the same time make sure that every Armenian and Assyrian knows that they are a second-class citizen. There is always the possibility they will face more intimidation. Intimidation has long been the policy of the government towards the newer Protestant churches because they all have members who used to be Muslims. This has infuriated the government.

In 1990, the Bible Society was closed down, and it is now completely illegal to print any Scriptures in Persian. This means all Bibles must be printed abroad and smuggled in, or printed secretly inside. For those receiving smuggled Scriptures, or those printing, the punishment can be very severe if they are found out. It is the same for all other Christian literature and resources: it is illegal to produce them in Persian which means again that the supply for Christians is very limited, relying on either secret presses or smuggling. It is possible to print some Christian titles legally in Iran if the government authorities can be persuaded that they are essentially academic and are in no way seeking to convert people.

The government has also banned these overground churches from having any conferences or Bible camps. Before the revolution there was a summer season of conferences for these Christians, but now they must travel abroad which has proved too expensive for many. Also it is impossible for any of the overground churches to run residential Bible Schools to train new leaders. They do run night classes, but these are closely watched by the government.

So because of government policies these churches are denied resources, conferences, training opportunities – and they are certainly not allowed to organize any evangelistic outreach, nor are they allowed to preach the gospel to all. The government constantly insists that only Christians are allowed into the services and so at a number of churches Muslims cannot attend unless specially invited. And many pastors have been presented with documents to sign where they promise not to have Muslims in their services. Some sign, others risk their lives and refuse.

Fearing the conversion of Muslims and that the church might act as a fifth column, the government constantly gathers information about church activities. It is very normal for Christian leaders to have their phones tapped and it has been known that one of them had two full-time members of the security services assigned to tracking his every movement. Nearly every week, leaders of the overground church are called into meet with officials from the Ministry of Information and though the Christians have to give a report on their church activities, very often they will be asked about their personal lives.

The government though does more than collect information and interview people. Over the years they have arrested many Christians and held them for questioning. One old lady simply brought back a Bible from abroad and gave it to an acquaintance. She was called in, told to sit facing a white wall and write as much as she knew about this aquaintance. When she entered that office she did not know how long she would have to stay. Another common tactic is to restrict people's travel. Passports will be confiscated or just not issued, or people will be made *Mamnu ol Khorooj*, which means their names go on a list which is given to all the port authorities who stop them from leaving the country.

And every Iranian Christian knows that whether you are originally from a historical Christian community or from a Muslim background, if you step over a line, you could be murdered. Stepping over that line for those from a Muslim background is becoming a Christian leader. So Reverend Sayyah, Reverend Soodmand, "Ravanbaksh", Ghorbandordi Tourani – all have been murdered. And stepping over that line for an Armenian is if they embarrass or challenge the government. This is what the Armenian Reverend Haik Hovsepian-Mehr did when he campaigned for the release of Muslim convert Mehdi Dibaj who had been sentenced to death for apostasy. In 1994, Haik Hovsepian-Mehr was abducted, stabbed to death, and thrown into a Muslim grave. He was later buried in a Christian Cemetery.

It is not fair to suggest that the government has persecuted Christians on either the same scale or with the same vicious cruelty as the atheistic communist powers; however, they have now maintained a high level of menacing, and sometimes murderous, intimidation against Christians for over twenty-five years.

This intimidation has been most intense in the provincial cities and, by and large, the government has been successful. Overground congregations are made up almost entirely of either Armenians or Assyrians who have become Protestant, or with older people who were Christians before the revolution. And in some places, like Kerman, the church has closed down all together.

In Tehran the overground churches have proved more resilient at dealing with the intimidation. This is partly due to the strength of leadership of the churches, partly due to the authorities being aware of the international diplomatic presence, and the fact that Tehran is such a massive city the police have other things on their minds. So quite a number of Muslims will find their way into services in the capital. However the government has intimidated the Assemblies of God church in Tehran. In September 2004 they arrested the entire leadership while they were conducting an annual business meeting. All of those arrested were told they were not allowed to evangelize or have Muslims in their churches. There is no doubt that many in the new government would want the churches in Tehran to wither away.

As well as the political intimidation, all the members of these churches have to cope with the economic restrictions that face all Christians in Iran. It is extremely difficult for Christians to find work and, with unemployment already running at nearly 15 per cent and set to rise, this will get a lot worse. And if a Muslim becomes a Christian and this is discovered they are nearly always fired, and their children can be expelled from school. Again the message to Christians is "there is no future for you or your families in this Islamic Republic", and so there has also been an exodus of Protestant Christians to the West.

So this is what government policy means to over-ground Christians at street level. They cannot have a normal church life, they cannot have the resources or training they need, and they certainly cannot evangelize. And all the time they have to be looking over their shoulder, because somebody could well be watching them with hostile intent. Just as the government has wanted, most have concluded there is no future for them or their families and have either left or are planning to leave.

There is, though, a third type of church in Iran, simply known as the underground church. Nobody knows exactly how many networks there are, or how many groups and members there are in each network, but one network has at least a thousand members.

This church is the result of the government policy. Seeing that it was impossible to build a healthy church overground with all the intimidation and harassment this attracted, leaders have decided to go totally underground. The character of the underground church is completely different from the overground one. The identity of believers is fiercely protected and they will often use given names, even with one another. They will regularly change their meeting place so as not to arouse the suspicion of their neighbors who might inform on them, and this will also influence the volume of their worship. Most of these believers will have absolutely no contact with the overground churches, though they might receive help from an Iranian pastor from outside the country, or they will rely on the teaching from satellite TV or the internet.

This church has really been emerging in just the last five years. It is the direct result of the government making Iran a closed land, and it might become one of the historical turning points of the Middle East. For this church is very active and when its members go out to share they meet many open hearts. For despite all the hostility of the government and all the pressure this puts on the church, Iranians in this generation are very open to hearing about Jesus Christ.

It is to this that we now turn.

OPEN HEARTS

Given the hostility of the government and the way
they have choked church activity, one would expect
to hear that the number of Muslims becoming
Christians has declined. It is the exact opposite. The
numbers have dramatically risen; indeed, more
Iranian Muslims have become Christian since the
1979 revolution than at any other time in Iran's history as an Islamic nation. Despite all the pressures
the churches have faced, still hundreds of Muslims
have tried to find out about Jesus Christ from the
overground churches. In the Assemblies of God central church in Tehran, where many meet every week,
people will come forward for prayer even before the
preacher has finished. No government informer can
stop that happening. And it is obvious that the
underground church networks are growing all the
time. For a movement to grow from a few members
to over one thousand members in less than five
years is absolutely unprecedented in Iran. No

church has ever grown that fast in Iran in modern history.

Having read about the hostility of the government, you might ask, why are these new Christians not arrested and charged with apostasy. And the answer is that the government does not easily find out. Their informers tend to focus on known Christian activists, and if the families of the converts are not fanatical they will not report the conversion. If they are fanatical, then the new convert would not tell them. Another reason is that even in the government, as the story of the European on the plane to Tehran shows, there are many who are uneasy about implementing the death sentence for apostates, which means that even if they did know someone was an apostate, they might not want to arrest the new Christians and put them on trial for their life, so inevitably attracting a lot of public attention. So, as long as the apostate keeps very quiet, then they might well be left alone.

So, careful new Christians can survive in Iran – but why are there so many new Christians in this closed country? Why are Iranians so open?

There are at least three reasons: Iranians are deeply disillusioned with the Islamic government; they have a strong awareness of their non-Islamic identity; and they have been attracted by the witness of the church.

Open Factor 1: Disillusionment with Islamic government

There was optimism, hope and celebration in the air when Ayatollah Khomeini arrived in Iran in February 1979 to set up the world's first ever modern Islamic theocracy. This has turned to bitter disillusionment for millions because Khomeini did not bring hope, prosperity and freedom, but war, economic chaos and totalitarianism.

War with Iraq

When Iraq invaded Iran in September 1980, it seemed quite clear that Saddam Hussein was the aggressor, and some Iranians believed the Americans were also involved.[1] In fact, Khomeini was a major factor in starting this war. As soon as he came to power, he encouraged the majority Shi'a population in Iraq to throw off Saddam's rule and establish an Islamic Republic. When Saddam asked for the old man to back down, Khomeini not only heightened the rhetoric, but also supported Shi'a assassination squads in Iraq who nearly managed to murder Saddam's deputy, Tariq Aziz. Saddam, essentially a jungle animal, came to the conclusion that the only way to get the ayatollah off his back was to invade and topple him first – as well as incorporating the neighboring

Iranian province of Khuzestan, with its oil and Arab-speaking population, into Iraq.[2]

Saddam's invasion was a gift for Khomeini, for there is nothing like an external enemy to unite a country. All Iranians wanted to defend their land, and hundreds of thousands of volunteers set off willingly to the frontline. This is still true today; there is no disillusionment about defending the motherland. But this war did not stay a war of defense. By May 1982 Iran had driven the Iraqis from their territory, and Saddam Hussein offered a ceasefire. But Khomeini did not want peace and for the next six years hundreds of thousands of Iranians died in Iraqi territory.

But what were they dying for, now the enemy had been driven from the homeland? They were dying for Khomeini's brand of pan-Islamism which he believed should spread over the whole world, starting with Baghdad, and then moving onto Jerusalem. If he had managed to free Iran from the curse of secularism and heathen Westernization, surely God now wanted him to free others. And surely one should start in one's own territory, with Saddam's secular regime, as well as Saudi Arabia, Kuwait and the Gulf States whose leaders were like the Shah, poodles of the West selling the soul of Islam for carnal pleasures. For Khomeini, foreign policy was not about countries, but about religion: "God has decreed for us the duty of fighting these opponents of Islam and of the Islamic nation."[3]

Saddam Hussein was so nervous that Iran would continue the war into Iraq in 1982 that he ordered the assassination of Sholov Argov, the Israeli ambassador in London, in the hope this would trigger Israel's invasion of Lebanon.[4] At the same time he would offer to unite with Khomeini to rid Muslims lands of the crusader state. Israel did invade Lebanon, and Khomeini did announce his intention to capture Jerusalem, but he would do it via Baghdad.[5] Khomeini was determined to rid the region of Saddam. His hatred for him was obsessive, so towards Iraq the policy was always "War, War till Victory".

This second phase of the war to liberate Baghdad was a disaster for Iran militarily and morally. Militarily, the defenses inside Iraq were very strong. The Iranians were unable to either attack them from the air or with accurate artillery, so, like in Europe's First World War, all advances had to be by waves of infantry. And just as in the First World War, the infantry were cut to pieces by machine guns. Sometimes the Iranians would break through the first line of defense, only to be trapped by a second.

Morally the war was a disaster. Khomeini's hardcore supporters believed his fantasy rhetoric about liberating Jerusalem via Baghdad, but most Iranians found it hard to understand the aim of the war now Iran was safe. The bloodshed seemed unnecessary.

The morality of the war became even more repugnant when in 1982 Khomeini encouraged young boys to offer themselves as martyrs on the frontline. When asked whether parents needed to give their permission, Khomeini's reply was: "So long as forces are needed at the war fronts, serving there is a religious duty and there is no need for parental consent."[6] So mullahs were sent to the schools to recruit and give plastic keys which would guarantee the child martyrs entrance into paradise. These children were used as mine sweepers or formed a part of the human wave attacks that were always, not surprisingly, repulsed. Here is how one Iraqi officer described these children attacks

> Once we had Iranian kids on bikes cycling towards us and my men all started laughing, and then these kids all started lobbing their hand grenades and we stopped laughing and started shooting.[7]

As Iranians brooded over this pointless slaughter on the frontline, they also had to deal with the frightening fact that Saddam Hussein had started to use nerve gas and other chemical weapons on their soldiers. It is estimated Iraq's chemical weapons caused 50,000 casualties.[8] And they had to live through Iraqi missile and air attacks on Iran's cities, which caused 30 per cent of Tehran's population to flee, and killed thousands.[9] As well as the horrific violence of the war, there was its devastating impact on the economy. The war cost $160 billion[10] and drove the already faltering post-revolutionary economy into depression, resulting in chronic shortages of basic necessities.

The war tormented all Iranians. Nearly every family had a friend or a relative who had been killed or injured by the war, and every family saw their living standards plummet. And what was this war for? It was all for Khomeini's Islam and dreams about taking over the whole Muslim world. And as he drank his famous cup of poison and gave permission for his lieutenants to negotiate a ceasefire with Saddam in 1988, what had Iran gained from the war? The answer staring at every Iranian was painfully obvious: absolutely nothing.

Such needless suffering has caused the majority of Iranians to become deeply disillusioned with the regime that gave them the war, and with the religion in whose name the war was fought.

Twenty years later, bereaved families still visit the graves of Islam's young soldiers and look at their faces staring back from fading photographs. And many ask whether the true God would really want to take twelve-year-olds and blow them up. Once the Iranian doubts Khomeini's verdict on this, then all his verdicts about Islam become questionable. And so the ordinary Iranian becomes more open to other ideas about God, and they are especially attracted to a Prophet who never waged war, told his followers to "turn the other cheek", and declared God's blessing on the peacemakers.

War inside Iran

Khomeini arrived in Tehran on February 1 1979; by February 8, he had won complete control of Iran; and on February 15, the executions started.[11] They have never finished.

The start of this war against the internal enemies of the revolution began with the generals and leaders of the Shah's regime. Right from the start, Khomeini relied on Ayatollah Sadeq Khalkhali to carry out revolutionary justice. Khalkhali, who had absolutely no legal training at all, would perform the role of prosecutor, judge and jury, believing he represented the views of all the Iranian people: "I issued judgment and acted as the conscience of 35 million people".[12] Khomeini and his entourage first ruled from the Refah Girls School in Tehran and here Khalkhali turned a classroom into a makeshift court. Once the sentence of execution was given, the condemned were taken to the roof of the school and shot.

Perhaps, in the early days, few tears were shed as leaders of the Shah's notorious SAVAK were despatched, but soon his enthusiasm for summary executions earned him the title the "Hanging Judge". In the first year and a half of the revolution, he oversaw the executions of at least fifteen hundred people, most of them royalists. None of them would have had access to a defense lawyer, as according to Khalkhali: "There is no room in the Revolutionary Courts for defence lawyers because they keep quoting laws to play for time."[13] Later, Khalkhali was sent to deal with opposition among the Kurds on whom Ayatollah Khomeini had declared a holy war. Sometimes up to sixty Kurds a day would be executed by Khalkhali's itinerant courts.

An example of his cavalier approach is illustrated by how he dealt with one defendant whose father was a usurer. "What does my father's crime have to do with me?" protested the accused. "Usury is *haram* – sin," thundered Khalkhali, "and so is the seed of usury. Kill him! Next."[14]

One day after finishing his work, Khalkhali was told that he had sent an innocent fourteen-year-old boy to his death. Khalkhali replied that he was not worried because if the boy was indeed innocent he had sent him to paradise.

Khalkhali eventually became too embarrassing for Iran's first president Bani-Sadr and was retired in December 1980. He had outraged the whole world when he was shown on television prodding the charred bodies of the US helicopter pilots who had died trying to rescue the embassy hostages; and then, while dealing with drug traffickers with his usual zeal, millions of dollars went missing from the official accounts.

Though Khalkhali was sidelined, he had still successfully established the precedents of how the new revolutionary regime would deal with its enemies: the faithful would "dispense with troublesome formalities",[15] and the regime would use the executions to maximize fear among the people. Khalkhali would often organize for eight people to be hanged at once from cranes so everyone could see the dangling corpses.

Khalkhali was more than embarrassing; he was mentally sick. It is well known that he had spent time as a child in a psychiatric ward and it was rumored that his favorite hobby was strangling cats. Yet it was Ayatollah Khomeini who had allowed this cruel and mentally depraved man to indiscriminately kill thousands of alleged enemies of the revolution. It is not possible to separate Khomeini from any of Khalkhali's brutality, as is made very clear in an interview Khalkhali gave to the French newspaper *Le Figaro*. Asked if he should be charged with crimes against humanity, his reply was: "No. It is not possible. If I had acted wrongly, Imam Khomeini would have told [me]. I only did what he asked me to do."[16] And Khomeini too did not hide the fact that he

approved of summary executions: "Criminals should
not be tried," he once said, "the trial of criminals is
against human rights. Human rights demand that we
should have killed them in the first place when it
became known they were criminals."[17]

After dealing with the royalists, the regime
moved on to deal with the Mojahadeen and the communists. Founded in 1965, the Mojahadeen was an
Islamic socialist party that had been more fiercely
involved in the campaign to rid Iran of the Shah
than many of the radical mullahs. For a while
Khomeini worked with them, but once he began to
establish his own power, he let his instinctive suspi-
cions about them be known. They were "eclectics"
contaminated by the "Western plague", hypocrites
and unbelievers. Faced with this hostility, the
Mojahadeen began to campaign against the new
regime. Well organized and attracting possibly 20
per cent of the country's support,[18] mainly from the
young, educated, religiously minded, they were a
serious threat to Khomeini. He met them with violence. When on June 20 1981 half a million demon-
strated against the regime, thousands were arrested,
and some were summarily executed on the spot.[19]
The Mojhadeen reacted by assassinations and ter-
rorist attacks, the worst being a bomb at the head-
quarters of the regime's political party which killed
seventy-four[20] revolutionary leaders.

The government reaction was furious. As Khomeini urged families to spy on each other and to hand over anyone with the faintest of connections with the Mojahadeen, thousands were arrested and, by the end of 1981, Amnesty International estimated over two thousand five hundred were tried and executed in the Khalkhali fashion.[21] The Mojahadeen, whose leadership fled first to Paris and then Iraq, claimed that between June 1981–April 1982 at least twelve thousand were killed by the regime.[22]

This war of terror against the Mojahadeen brutalized Iran, with nearly every neighborhood knowing of an arrest or an execution. In one city, people tell of a young revolutionary guard who arrived one morning at a quiet middle-class home, with flowers in his hand. He gave them to the mother of the house saying that the night before he had become her *Damad* (son-in-law). He meant he had raped her daughter so that before her execution she did not die a virgin and go to heaven. There is also the story of a mother who handed her son over to the authorities – and watched his execution. Or there is the judge who sentenced his own son to execution.

Founded in 1920, The Iranian Communist Party (Tudeh) was much older than the Mojahadeen – and seemingly more threatening, as they were supported by the Soviet Union. At the start of the revolution, the Tudeh party, like all the other left-wing groups, supported Khomeini against the Shah. When Khomeini began his attack on the Mojahadeen, the Tudeh party decided to collaborate with the clerical regime. They claimed that Khomeini deserved their support as he was against imperialism and used a lot of their anti-capitalist rhetoric. The real reason was that they wanted to become the dominant party of the left. In 1981, the regime was happy to work with them, as they helped expose Mojahadeen cells to the Revolutionary Guards. The turn of the Tudeh party came when they criticized Khomeini's policy of continuing the war inside Iran. The whole party was accused of being spies and the agent of a foreign power. The leadership were arrested, but strangely spared execution; a fate suffered by many of the 5,000 party foot soldiers.[23]

By the summer of 1983, Khomeini had won the internal war with nearly all the leaders and members of the royalists, Mojahadeen, and communists either dead, in exile or in prison. And five years later, in response to a Mojahadeen attack from Iraq, the regime killed most of those who had been imprisoned in 1981. A three-man committee, which included Iran's present Interior Minister, Mustafa Pour-Mohammad, visited all the country's prisons and, Khalkhali-style, tried and executed thousands of political prisoners.[24] The international community was appalled. As have been the vast majority of Iranians ever since Khalkhali introduced revolutionary justice to Iran. They are not just appalled, they are deeply disillusioned for Khalkhali was an ayatollah; his successors are the senior clergy and their overall inspiration was Imam Khomeini. And these clergymen have arrested, tortured and executed thousands of young people in the name of Islam.

This has made millions question Islam and attracted them to Jesus Christ. For while Khomeini lashed out in revenge against his enemies, even appointing a maniac like Khalkhali, Jesus Christ told his followers to pray for their enemies, and he forgave those who tortured and killed him. It is this contrast which has made so many Iranians open to the gospel.

War, external and internal, has made Iranians disillusioned with their Islamic government. There are two other factors that have also made Iranians question Islam – the economy and personal liberty.

Economic chaos

In the 1960s and for much of the 1970s, Iranians enjoyed a massive increase in their standard of living. Certainly there was still an elitist land-owning class, and there was a class of poor agricultural laborers tied to the land, but there was also a very fast-growing middle class who enjoyed comfortable houses, television, luxury cars, foreign holidays, and sending their children abroad for further education. The revolution then arrived and sent Iran's economy into disarray, with the middle classes being the hardest hit.

A part of Ayatollah Khomeini's attack on the Shah was the royal family's extravagant lifestyles, epitomized by their celebrations to commemorate 2,500 years of the Iranian monarchy which were held at Persepolis in 1971. Here an air-conditioned tent city was constructed to host foreign guests, who ate food cooked by Maxim's from Paris, off dinner plates designed by Limoges. Critics said it cost over $200 million.[25] In contrast, the lifestyle of Ayatollah Khomeini was very simple. He just owned an old house in Qom, and when he died his only other assets were very personal items like glasses, his turban and books. He did not even own the carpets in his room.[26]

This antipathy for extravagance, the constant condemnation of greedy Western capitalists, and Khomeini's early rash promises of free water and electricity sometimes gave the impression that Robin Hood had come to power in Tehran.[27]

With this emotional approach, the instincts of the new regime were to nationalize, and this is what happened on a grand scale. All major industries, banks, and other businesses were taken over by the state, and Islamic foundations, known as *bonyads*, took over all the assets of the Shah and the royalists. This meant that Khomeini's regime had massive economic power and it used at least 20 per cent of the country's income to subsidize transport and food for the masses, and to reward its hardline supporters.

It also had many economic problems, especially in the 1980s. Strict US sanctions not only severely restricted Iran's exports, but also meant much of the country's industrial infrastructure was crippled, as it depended on US spare parts. There was also a major drain of capital from the country as investors were completely uncertain of the new regime's economic competency. The war then decimated the country's economy – as well its actual cost, there was the horrendous damage Iraq inflicted on all of Iran's major economic assets, especially the oil refinery in Abadan which was virtually destroyed. In 1985, oil prices then plummeted and, with Iran's economy depending almost entirely on the black gold for foreign currency, the regime was starved of much-needed income. Finally, by the mid 1980s, the regime's nationalization program was absorbing up to 80 per cent of the country's economic activity into the state. And with nationalization came all the normal time-consuming bureaucracy, inefficiency, and corruption associated with state-run businesses. An example of the frustrating bureaucracy an investor might face is well illustrated by the fact that to obtain a confirmation of a letter of credit from a bank involves up to twenty procedures involving three ministries and five departments from the Central Bank. And ultimately, as happened in the early 1980s, the state can step in at any time and either change the rules or nationalize any industry or business they want to, and decide on what compensation, if any, should be given to investors.

The regime's economic policies brought chaos and humiliation for Iranians. At home, inflation was rampant, often running at between 40 per cent and 50 per cent, so for many families the only topic of conversation was the rising price of basic necessities. And then, after the inflation, came the shortages. Paper had to be rationed; soap was difficult to find; there were even long lines for gasoline and bread. With Iran owning around 10 per cent of the world's oil reserves this brought many sharp comments from critics. And abroad, the Iranians who travelled to the few countries who gave them visas easily, found that tomans that used to produce so many dollars, hardly produced any.[28]

In the 1990s, the economy improved. The end of the war lessened government expenditure and encouraged investors back. President Rafsanjani, understanding the stifling nature of excessive state ownership, brought more freedom into the economy which encouraged business life. And, most importantly of all, oil prices began to improve in 1994.

However, the handling of the economy is still a major issue for Iranians. Unemployment is rising, and many believe the mullahs have got rich on the back of ordinary Iranians. At the start of the revolution Ayatollah Khomeini called on people to have large families. The people responded and there was a massive baby boom in the 1980s. As a consequence, Iran's population is now one of the youngest in the world with 75 per cent being under twenty-five. So in the late 1990s there was an acute lack of work and to ease the situation the state has created thousands of jobs which are subsidized by the profits from oil. Official government figures put the unemployment rate at 13 per cent, but experts say it is a lot more, and predict that in the next few years it will rise dramatically when the state can no longer afford to subsidize jobs. The dearth of employment has been particularly bad for graduates as there are nowhere near enough suitable vacancies for them. The excess of available labor keeps wages very low, while inflation continues to force prices up, and so it is common for many breadwinners in Iranian households to have both a day and an evening job to make ends meet.[29]

Others who cannot find extra work often turn to drugs to dull the pain of their empty days. Heroine is cheap and plentiful and with up to four million users, Iran has a massive drug problem. The rise in unemployment also seems a direct cause in the staggering rise in prostitution. Estimates say there are 300,000 girls working in Tehran alone, some as young as fourteen.

While ordinary Iranians struggle to earn a living wage and see friends sink into drug addiction, they believe the insiders of the regime are making millions. The man who symbolizes the corruption many fear operates at the heart of the regime is Hashemi Rafsanjani. From his many years in the corridors of power he now has a personal fortune that is reputed to be over one billion US dollars. It is estimated that other clergy in the present government have assets worth between three to six hundred million US dollars.[30]

As well as their own business interests, it is the clergy who control the bonyads, the Islamic foundations which initially took over all of the wealth of the Shah and his followers to spread economic justice. They are now some of the largest economic complexes not just in Iran, but in the Middle East. The Foundation for the Oppressed and War Veterans controls an estimated $12 billion in assets. As well as owning thousands of factories with nearly half a million workers, they own shipping lines, Iran's largest soft drink company, chemical plants, and a lot of property. The foundation that administers all the wealth that pours into the shrine of Imam Reza in Mashad has an annual budget of over $2 billion and controls most of the economy in Khorasan, a large province in the north-east of Iran. Much of the wealth of these foundations is because they are given special help from the regime, so, for example, they can borrow money at half the rate of interest from the Central Bank as other businesses. And if their interests are seriously threatened, then their influence with the regime is such that they can easily ward off competitors. As these foundations are essentially personal fiefdoms of ayatollahs and mullahs, their activities and the government's often merge, so really they operate above the law. They do not submit audited accounts; and they ignore tax, currency and tariff laws.[31]

Another group with very close ties to the government are the bazaaris, the men, and there are only men, who run the bazaars in the centre of all of Iran's major cities and towns. Throughout Iran's history, the bazaaris have had a close relationship with the mosque. They have always stood for very conservative values, and detested the Shah's flirting with Western fashion. Furthermore, they were completely sidelined by the Shah's economic policies and they saw their incomes fall in the early 1970s. So, after the mullahs, they were Ayatollah Khomeini's most natural supporters, distributing his taped sermons, and always responding to his calls for strikes against the Shah.

After the success of the revolution they certainly shared in the country's economic difficulties, but there is an unproven assumption that they have been protected more than the rest of the people. The bazaar is very much a closed society. They help each other and are suspicious of outsiders. So it is assumed, as the nation's wholesalers, they not only looked after each other during the war years, but also hoarded to push prices even higher. The accounting in the bazaar is not at all transparent; indeed, if you wander around any of them you will notice that the traders do not seem to have computers. This is because no *bazaari* likes to pay taxes, so they do not like accurate records. However much profit they have made, they always want to give the impression that business is bad. They have an expression which says, "You have five fingers, but only show four of them. Always hide one finger." And the government has been more than prepared to tolerate this.[32]

The economy has caused a lot of suffering for Iranians. Living standards have crumbled, and families have been broken up as young men go in search of work. The Revolutionary Government has a history of trying to blame foreigners for internal suffering, but the present regime has had its hands on the levers of power for too long for this blame-shifting to be credible. For while ordinary Iranians have faced soaring inflation, low wages and unemployment, the insiders of the regime – those in government, those administering the *bonyads*, the *bazaaris* – have clearly grown rich. This feeling was summed up during the

1999 student demonstrations in Tehran when the crowd chanted, "The mullahs have become God and the people have become poor."[33]

By naming the mullahs, the students were expressing a widespread view that they are corrupt. Yet it is these very same mullahs who again and again have been claiming to bring the government of Islam to the country. And so the disillusionment with the corrupt mullahs spreads to disillusionment with Islam. This is now exacerbated by access to the internet where young Iranians can easily see what their contemporaries enjoy in the West. They are no less intelligent than the Europeans or the Americans, and they live in a country with massive oil and gas reserves, yet their living standards are much lower than their Western counterparts. Twenty-five years ago, Iranians successfully blamed the wicked foreign capitalist: now they blame the mullahs and Islam.

So, Iranians are disillusioned with Islam because under the regime they have experienced war and economic chaos. They have also experienced unprecedented interference in their private lives.

Totalitarianism

During the 2006 World Cup in Germany, visiting Iranians were asked to name the most important change they wanted to see in their country. Most replied with one word: *"Azadi"* – freedom. Tragically, of course, this is what most of the Iranians wanted when they poured onto the streets in 1979 to welcome Ayatollah Khomeini: what they ended up with was a religious dictatorship. For Khomeini not only made sure he controlled all political and economic power, but also gave the new religious state the right to interfere in the details of people's lives.

From the first days of the revolution, it was clear that women were not going to be allowed to live freely. From the age of nine, all Iranian females in public must wear a scarf, which should be worn in a way so not a single piece of hair is showing. They must also wear either a loose-fitting coat called a *manteau*, or even better a *chador*, a black cloth which covers the lady from head to foot. And, however hot the weather, they must wear socks, even at the beach. Though they do, women are also not meant to wear excessive make-up, or smoke or swim in public. The whole rationale behind these regulations is that women must not appear independent or attractive to other men. This rationale also means there must be segregation in public and couples in the street can be challenged to prove that they are family. This segregation operates in schools, in a lot of colleges, and also in sport. It causes a lot of frustration for female soccer fans as they are not allowed to attend live games.[34] At the beach they also lose out, for while men can swim at all beaches, women can only swim in designated areas where a high canvas wall curtains off a special female-only area. Men's dress has not been left completely alone by the revolutionary authorities. They are not meant to wear shorts or short-sleeved shirts, and ties are definitely frowned on. They are Western.

Entertainment and the media are strictly controlled. Of course, all alcohol, clubbing and gambling is banned. In the early days of the revolution, the new regime was so fanatical that all music was made illegal, along with playing cards, backgammon – and even chess! Television is operated by the state; all books and magazines must get permission before they are published; films are routinely censored; and, though it is a Herculean task for the government, pornographic and overtly political websites are blocked.

Newspapers are even more tightly controlled. There was a slight lessening of restrictions on the press when Khatami came to power in 1997. But conservatives soon made their will known and a number of intellectuals and journalists were killed in 1998 – and many "reformist" newspapers, sometimes twenty each month, were closed down. As well as blocking some websites, the government has also pursued "bloggers" who are particularly critical of the regime, and given them prison sentences.[35]

Though Islamic rule is the norm in public, it is often said that in private Iranians are surprisingly free. Regarding dress – visitors will comment on how ladies will enter their home, take off their *chadors* or *manteaus*, and be wearing the most glamorous Paris fashions underneath. Regarding entertainment – Iranians can generally obtain any Western film or music they want on DVD or CD and they can watch thousands of different programs on their satellite TVs. And there is plenty of alcohol available on the black market for those who want to drink, for as one writer has said, "there are just too many good grapes grown in Iran."[36] Indeed, people joke that the only industry Iran is completely self-sufficient in is alcohol production. There is even more heroin and opium available.

However, this private freedom is never certain. Fanatical vigilante groups sent by the local *Komitehs* can appear at any time of day or night to confiscate satellite dishes, or arrest people in their homes for un-Islamic behaviour. Stories of their meddling abound, especially with weddings. Iranians love a good wedding, and this has always traditionally meant dancing. But mixed dancing is taboo in public, and most Iranians have to hire a hotel for their reception as there are so many guests. So what often happens is that guests will go to the hotel for a segregated meal, but will then gather later in a large private home to dance the night away. The local *Komiteh* often gets a tip-off about this – or perhaps neighbors phone up – and seven or eight of their agents will turn up threatening to arrest everyone for immoral behavior. This soon dampens the party spirit as people in Iran have been sentenced to death for sexual immorality, and also for drinking alcohol if they are caught three times.

In Iran, sex before marriage, adultery and homosexuality are all illegal, with punishments ranging from 100 lashes, to the guilty being stoned to death. The normal rule is that for the first conviction the punishment is lashes, but on the third it is the death sentence. However, the judge often chooses to use the death sentence earlier. In 2005, a young teenage girl and two young men were sentenced to 100 lashes for having sex; two years earlier, there was international outrage when Leyla Mafi was sentenced to death for prostitution – even though she is said to have a mental age of eight. Her case is still being reviewed.[37] In 2006, nine women and two men were sentenced to death by stoning for adultery.[38] Homosexuals have definitely been executed, some say in large numbers.[39] In 2005, two teenagers in Mashad were hanged. The authorities claimed they had raped a thirteen-year-old boy, but many believe it was because they were homosexual. It is the same rule for drinking alcohol – lashes for the first two convictions,

death for the third. So in June 2006, a Kurd, Karim
Fahimi, was condemned to die for this crime.[40]

It would be unfair to suggest that vigilante groups
are constantly entering people's homes, but the fact
that they can and sometimes do, and the fact that they
can punish with such draconian ferocity, causes
intense resentment among ordinary Iranians. And
again it is Islam that people see as being the root
cause of the problem, for these moral police are
knocking on their doors in the name of that religion.

But then what often happens at the door makes
people even *more* disillusioned with Islam. For the
father of the bridegroom, who has already paid out a
fortune for the wedding, will ask, in a very round-
about way, how much it will cost for the vigilantes
not to enter. And usually there is a price.

So, you have the followers of Islam wanting to stop
the celebration of a wedding, but if they are paid
enough, they will go away. This is the experience of
ordinary people and it makes them very disenchan-
ted with Islam. They wonder whether God really
does want his servants to go around upsetting
newlyweds, or taking bribes not to; and when they
conclude "no", it makes them question their faith,
and so open to others.

And, of course, when they do begin to explore
other religions, they meet this same totalitarianism.
For, as drinking and immorality are illegal, so too is

exploring another religion which might lead them to abandon Islam. Again it would be unfair to suggest that the authorities are constantly searching houses for Bibles and Christian literature, or, for that matter, material from other religions like Zoroastrianism. But the fact that Iranians risk the possible wrath of a *Komiteh* if they do start exploring other religions is by itself offensive. It might well be that many of them would like to remain in the religion of their birth – but most of them would certainly like the opportunity to consider the claims of other religions, and the fact that their government treats them like children and does not give them this freedom, further increases their antipathy towards the regime.

Totalitarianism means that the government can intrude into the details of a day. It might not be a constant experience, but over the years incidents have built up, pushing people to the edge. A few years ago, a Western family went to the Caspian Sea for a holiday. Once, when the Western family were swimming in the sea, they saw two Revolutionary Guards order a very young Iranian girl to get out – her swimming in front of family and friends was un-Islamic. The next day, the Western family noticed that she was sitting on the hot beach in her scarf and *manteau*, watching her brother and male cousins swim. For the Western family this was strange, a story to take home to tell others; but for the Iranian family it was a bitter reminder of being ruled by a religious regime that could step into a family holiday and force a young girl to stop swimming.

Since coming into power in 1979, the Iranian government has ruled for the glory of Islam. This has brought the Iranian people both external and internal war which has killed hundreds of thousands, economic chaos which has caused crippling inflation, low wages, and severe unemployment for most but spectacular wealth to the regime's insiders, and a totalitarianism that throttles free expression and interferes in the private details of people's lives. One of Iran's great kings, Darius, prayed that God might save his people from foes, famine, and falsehood. Most Iranians believe that the Islamic regime has given them all three.

As well as being deeply disappointed with Islam, there is another major factor that makes Iranians very open to the Christian gospel. This is their strong non-Islamic identity.

Open Factor 2: **Non-Islamic identity**

The identity of some countries, such as Saudi Arabia or Pakistan, is completely linked to Islam. Saudi Arabia is known throughout the world as the birthplace of Islam and the guardian of the religion's holy sites. To be Saudi is to be Muslim. Likewise, Pakistan was founded as a homeland for the Muslims of the subcontinent. Islam is the raison d'etre of the country's existence. So Saudis and Pakistanis and many other Muslims from other countries draw their historical, literary and religious identity from Islam. When they look in the mirror they say with pride they are Muslims, for Islam is central to their identities as Saudis or as Pakistanis. They have a lot more pride in their Islamic heritage than in their very newly created national identities.

Not so the Iranians. When they look in the mirror they are first and foremost proud of the fact that they are Iranian – *then* Muslim. They have a rich history stretching back long before the coming of Islam; they excel in a literary culture which, of course, is not Arabic; but often it is not strictly Islamic either. Even their version of Islam is very different from that of the vast majority of Muslims. In short, they have a strong non-Islamic identity and, as disillusionment with Islam grows, so too does interest in this non-Islamic identity. And this means that the Iranian, much more easily than the Saudi or Pakistani, can become Christian, as their being Iranian does not depend on Islam.

History

March is the happiest month in Iran: it is *No Ruz*, when all Iranians celebrate the New Year at the time

of the spring equinox. The celebration begins with a
major cleaning of the house – it is literally called a
"house shaking". This is followed by *Chahar-Shanbeh
Soori*, when on the last Wednesday night before the
New Year, people light small bonfires and jump
through them shouting "My yellow for you and your
red for me". Meanwhile, there has been a lot of shop-
ping – goldfish, sweets and new clothes are especially
in demand. The fish are for a special table known as
Haft Seen, where symbols of new life such as the fish
are placed along with seven other articles which all
begin with the letter *Seen* (S). Each article has a symbolic meaning, so for example the *sabzeh* – freshly
grown lentils – represents blessing for the crops. The
sweets are for the many family guests who will come
to visit, and the new clothes are another way of saying
the old has gone, the new has come.

The actual New Year is declared when astronomers
in Tehran sight the spring equinox. So rather than
waiting for a famous clock to strike midnight, as
Westeners do for their New Year, Iranian families sit
in front of a TV, or around a radio, waiting for this
official announcement. Then the party begins, and
the whole country closes down for nearly two weeks.
On the last day of the holiday, the thirteenth day,
everyone goes out into the countryside for a picnic
and to throw away the sabzeh that was grown for the
Haft Seen table, usually into a river. There is also a

tradition that says if an unmarried girl ties together the grass (grown from the lentil seed) into a bundle, then she will get married that year.

No Ruz is by far Iran's most important national celebration, and it has got nothing to do with Islam. The origins of the rituals reach back into Iran's early history, probably to the reign of Darius (522–486 BC), with some of the symbolic features being added later when Iran was officially a Zoroastrian country. Here we have a rich irony: the happiest time of year for the Islamic Republic is when Iranians celebrate a completely non-Islamic festival. Very aware of this, the new regime tried to ban the celebrations at the start of the revolution. But this was like the seventeenth-century Puritans trying to ban Christmas in England: it was impossible. So now the government disapproves but tolerates the festivities.

Every year *No Ruz* etches into the mind of all Iranians that they belong to an older culture than Islam's. This is reinforced by their love and respect for their ancient kings: 2,500 years ago Cyrus the Great established the Persian Empire, freed the Jews from their Babylonian captivity, and gave the world its first declaration of human rights. His successor, Darius, developed the world's fastest postal service, and built the magnificent Persepolis palace whose ruins still stand outside Shiraz. Other ancient Iranians excelled in mathematics, engineering and astronomy and are credited with the invention of irrigated farming. Every school child knows that Iran was the leading civilization of the ancient world and they know it was not created by Muslims. The message of history is simple: Iran's greatness does not depend on Islam.

Some would also look to history to make an even more controversial point. They would argue that Islam, originating in Arabia, with Arabic as its language, was forced on Iran in the seventh century and is essentially a foreign religion in the country. For Iranians are not Arab, they are Indo-European, and their mother tongue is not Arabic, but Persian. The Pahlavi kings tried to exploit this by attempting to develop a nationalist quasi religion. This ultimately failed, but still the message of Iran's greatness, independent of Islam, with this undertone that the religion was foreign, was instilled into the minds of their subjects and this has been passed on to their children.

Literature

There is a very popular parlor game in Iran called *Moshaereh*. The first player will quote a line of a poem, and then the next must quote a line of a poem which starts with the last letter of the last word of the previous player's verse. And so the game goes on till one of the players cannot quote a line. Most ordinary Westerners would not survive one or two rounds:

Iranians can play for hours. For an ordinary Iranian's speech is punctuated with poetry; it is a part of their life, constantly used in conversation to underline arguments, to tease, to point in another direction. Popular Iranian poets are nationally revered with shrines similar to religious prophets. Near Mashad is the tomb of Ferdowsi, the author of the epic *Shahname*; then in Shiraz there is the tomb of both Saadi and, probably Iran's most famous poet, Hafiz. At this shrine, people will kneel at the grave, and then they will pay money to have a poem of Hafiz picked for them in the belief this will hold a special message. This respect is also accorded to modern poets, seen by the tens of thousands who lined the streets of Tehran to honor the funeral cortege of Ahmad Shamlu, Iran's greatest modern poet, who died in July 2000. As he was borne on his final journey, so the crowd quoted from memory many lines of his poems.

All of Iran's great poets – Ferdowsi, Hafiz, Saadi, Rumi, Khayyam – were Muslims, but none of them made Islam their central theme. Ferdowsi was a nationalist whose passion was making sure the Persian language and glory of Iran's history survived the Arab invasion; Hafiz and Rumi were both mystics who deliberately expressed spiritual ideas with images which were taboo for orthodox Muslims; Saadi's main concern was practical morality, and

Khayyam was an Epicurean who satirized religious
people. So, though Persian poetry deals with the
divine, and certainly makes reference to Islam, on the
whole its tone is more universal, more questioning,
more enigmatic. When Iranians quote one of their
poets, they are taken to an intellectual landscape that
is not dominated by dogmatic Islamic absolutes, but
rather by a burning love for the Persian language and
humanity's universal quest for meaning. This not
only underlines the fact that Iran has a non-Islamic
identity, but it also means that some readers have
developed a mentality that is open to considering
other theological ideas.

Religion

It would seem absurd to argue that Iran has a separate religious identity to Islam when its population is
over 98 per cent Muslim. However, though the country might not have a separate religious identity, it certainly has a very different one to the rest of the
Islamic world. For with 85 per cent of the Muslim
world Sunni, Iran is the only country with an over-
whelming Shi'a majority – 89 per cent.[41] And it is the
only country in the world where the Shi'a faith is the
state religion. Add to this the fact that Sufism, the
mystic version of Islam, is very widespread in Iran,
and that all Iranians are aware that before the coming

of Islam their country was Zoroastrian, then it really is not absurd to say that Iran has a very different religious identity to the rest of the Muslim world.

Iran became Shi'a at the start of the sixteenth century in the aftermath of the Moguls' cruel and destructive invasion where entire cities were put to the sword. The new king, Ismail, was the first truly Iranian ruler the country had had since the Arabic invasions of the seventh century. To secure the loyalty of his people, he wanted to reject the Sunni religion of his rivals, the Turks and the Uzbeks, and establish Shi'a Islam as the country's faith. Ismail was very determined this should happen and got his officials to denounce Sunnis in all the country's public squares. Shi'a Islam became Iran's national religion, and this meant the culture of Iran impacted the religion, just as much as the religion impacted Iran. It is very similar to what happened to Christianity when English kings decided to assert their country's nationalism by creating their own and separating from Roman Catholic Europe, ruled by the Pope. Anglicanism is certainly rooted in the historical church, but it is also very English. In the same way the Shi'a faith is rooted in historical Islam, but it too is very Iranian. Indeed it can be argued that though superficially it looks as if Islam invaded Iran, what eventually happened was that Islam was adapted to Iran.

Shi'a Islam revolves around the first twelve Imams, the direct descendants of Mohammad, with especial focus on Ali, Mohammad's son-in-law, and his son Hussein, who were denied their right to rule the Muslims by the Sunnis.

This would seem to mean then that Iran's religious heroes were Arab which would not serve Ismail's nationalism. He had an answer. With breathtaking confidence, Ismail claimed that the very first Imam in the Shi'a faith, Ali, when searching for a wife for his second son, Hussein, did not go to the Arabs. He went to the Iranians. And the girl he found was none other than Shahrbanou, the daughter of the last Iranian Sasanian king, Yazdigird. Ismail was especially careful to make sure that the Iranian girl married Hussein, the great hero of the Shi'a faith who bravely fought for his legitimate rights against impossible odds at Karbala rather than give in as others had. With one alleged marriage, Ismail achieved a lot for Iranian nationalism. First of all, by having Ali come to the Iranians for his son's wife, he underlines the perception that Ali was semi-detached from the Arabs and more comfortable with the Iranians. Then, with the actual marriage, Ismail combines two of the most revered genealogies in the popular Iranian mind: the Sasanians and Mohammad's family. And, of course, now all the Imams after Hussein have Iranian blood.[42]

So the great heroes of the Shi'a faith, Ali and Hussein – Mohammad's son-in-law and grandson – have been absorbed into the greater Persian family. Not only do their pictures, always on sale at street stalls, seem to look more Iranian than Arab, but their suffering for justice has also merged into Iran's national story. So Ali, whom Mohammad said should be his successor, is denied the succession, just as Iran, clearly a great regional culture and power, has been denied her place in the sun by corrupt foreign elites. And Ali's reputation as a scholar and campaigner for the poor also merges with how, in Iran, the truly great ruler will never forget social justice.

Hussein's shadow over Iran is even greater than Ali's, for he is the man who willingly sacrificed himself for the Shi'a cause, rather than accept oppression. Though he clearly had a right to be the Caliph (leader of all Muslims) after the death of his father, the Sunni Ummayads in Damascus opposed him, and appointed Yezid. Hussein hoped to raise an army from Kufa, the Shi'a power base, but on his way there, at a place called Karbala, he and his companions were surrounded by a much larger Sunni army. Knowing it would be certain death to engage the Sunni army with just seventy-two men, Hussein still chose to fight as a matter of honor. The night before the battle at Karbala he wore a white funeral shroud, and the next day he was cut down and his body was trampled over by the Sunni horsemen. His skull was sent back to Damascus. This tragic tale has merged with Iran's national story as it has been remembered in street theatre and marches every year during the month of Moharram.[43] For just as Hussein's body was trampled over, so too has Iran's – by the Greeks, the Parthians, the Arabs, the Turks, the Moguls, the Russians, the British and, through the last Shah, by the Americans. It is no coincidence that it was during Moharram in December 1978 that violence against the Shah erupted to such a peak that he was convinced he had to leave. For the religious Iranian, it was as if the blood of Hussein was crying out from the fields of Karbala, literally driving him out.

Iran then has a different Islamic background because of the way Shi'a Islam has been adapted to the national story. It is also very different because of the prevalence of Sufism in Iran. Sufis are the mystics, the people who believe that God can be experienced intuitively. Outwardly they may be observers of the Shari'a Law, but their main concern is the inward journey. There are Sufis throughout the Islamic world, but many of the most important were Iranian. There was Hassan Basri, the radical ascetic from the eighth century; Mohammad Ghazali, who helped to reconcile the mystic and legal tradition; Al-Surawardi who founded the Illuminationist School in the twelfth century; and Molla Sadra, Iran's greatest philosopher, who built on Al-Surawardi's work in the seventeenth century, developing a system he called metaphilosophy. The impact of Sufism on Iran has been immense and inevitably changes the country's sense of religious identity. For as soon as Iranians begin to meditate on their own spiritual journey, they do not just think about the Koran and the Shari'a Law, but they are drawn to think about these great Iranian philosophers, and their great poets such as Rumi, Hafiz and Attar – who were all associated with Sufism.

The combination of the Shi'a faith and Sufism on Iran's religious identity is ironically one of the major reasons why Iranians are so open to the gospel of Jesus Christ. For in the Shi'a faith there are a number of clear links to central truths in the Christian faith that do not exist in Sunni Islam.

First of all, the Shi'as are primarily devoted to the Imams, especially Ali, Hussein, and Mahdi. So whereas the Sunnis look to the traditions handed down by the elders, the Shi'as look to heroic individuals and the examples they set. This is very similar to what Christians do: they are devoted primarily to the person of Jesus Christ, not a set of traditions or abstract doctrines.

And then, what the Imams have come to symbolize is not completely alien to Christianity. Ali is the simple-living ascetic who campaigned for the poor and Hussein is clearly a suffering savior, a righteous man who was ready to die for a cause. And indeed some scholars widen this out and say Hussein was in some ways dying for the sins of his people. The last Imam is the hidden one, Mahdi, and what he represents is also close to Christian thinking. First of all, he is now hidden, but he is also present, especially in special places, such as the Jamkaran Mosque. So while Hussein died, Mahdi is still alive. And he is going to return to judge the world and restore righteousness.

If you roll these three Imams into one you have a man devoted to the poor; who died for the sins of his people; but is now alive watching the faithful and will one day return in righteousness. You have a man very similar to Jesus Christ.

Then the Christians teach that this Jesus must be experienced, and here the prevalence of Sufism plays a crucial role. For the Sufis have taught all Iranians to be ready to experience God at an intuitive level – to feel him, and especially to feel his love. So first the Iranian hears a message about a man who reminds him a lot about the Imams he has been taught to revere, and then there is an invitation to experience an invisible presence, to be united with the divine, which is the goal of all Sufis.

Iranians have always had a non-Islamic identity, but they have not always been open to Christianity. What is crucially different in this generation is that never before have so many Iranians been so deeply disillusioned with Islam. As we have already seen, the war, the executions, the economic chaos, the total-itarianism have made millions conclude that God cannot support Shi'a Islam. Iranians cannot believe that God was either with Khalkhali as he ordered the execution of innocents, or with Khomeini as he encouraged children to go to the frontline to fight a war of aggression, or with Rafsanjani as his manage-ment of the economy made him vastly rich but many others desperately poor, or with Ahmadinejad as he and his followers still try to stop young girls swim-ming in the Caspian Sea.

Imagine now a typical Iranian hearing about Christianity, or being invited to a Christian meeting. The first reaction is not "No, that is impossible because I am a Muslim" but, fed up of the regime's Islam, they say, "Why not? I am Iranian, and our great civilization does not depend on Islam. What's more, my poets and philosophers were Sufis, always willing to experience the divine in different places." So they come and there they are struck by the joyful worship being offered to Jesus Christ. And as they learn more, they cannot help but be reminded of the Imams they have been taught to revere. There is something about this Galilean Man that is very attrac-tive. And then they hear from others about how God gave them dreams about a "man in white"[44] who they understood later to be Jesus. They hear of others who have been spoken to by Jesus. And they are not shocked; this is not alien to them, because the Sufi tradition in Iran has made them ready to experience the mystical and supernatural. Finally, they see people going forward to the front, some are crying, some fall on their faces, and the leader of the meeting declares that Jesus Christ is among the congregation. Iranians have been taught that Mahdi is hidden, but present at special meetings, so this language is not impossible for them. They can believe that Christ is there and so, when invited to experience him, they are ready. To sum up: disillusioned with Islam, a natural place for the Iranian to turn to for an experience of God is Christianity.

Though open to Christianity, it might be that they are put off due to the constant anti-Christian propaganda in the media. But this is not the case; the reputation of Christians in Iran is not badly scarred, and this brings us to the third major reason why, despite living under such a closed regime, Iranians are so open to the gospel.

Open Factor 3: **Witness of the church**

There has been a thriving church in Iran since at least the mid second century when the country was evangelized by Assyrians from Edessa. One famous church historian says that by 340 AD "the way to India (i.e. Iran) was strewn with bishoprics and monasteries."[45]

By the mid sixth century, the influence of the church was such that Christians were welcomed at court and some bishops were trusted friends of the emperor. Despite the Arab invasions of the seventh century and the much crueler Mongol terror of the thirteenth and fourteenth centuries, this Assyrian church has survived with her Patriarch based in Orumieh in the north of Iran.

The Armenian Church is also very old. As mentioned earlier, Armenian Orthodox Christians were first brought to Iran in the early seventeenth century by King Shah Abbas to help construct his new capital in Isfahan. They were allowed to build their own churches and practise their religion in a special area near the city called Julfa. They stayed in Iran and established a reasonable life for themselves. At the start of the twentieth century thousands of other Armenians fled to Iran to escape the genocide unleashed against them in Turkey. They too established themselves, and were allowed to practise their religion.

Though their numbers are dramatically decreasing as thousands emigrate, still the Armenian and Assyrian Christians have been a constant presence in Iranian life. They run their own businesses, many of their children go to government schools, and so most Iranians will have met them. And generally the impression these Christians leave has been very favorable. There are many stories of Muslims who have become Christians who trace the first stage of their spiritual journey back to contact with an Armenian or an Assyrian Christian. There is a true story about a Muslim who badly hurt an Armenian child in a traffic accident. In Iran the families can claim compensation – even life – so when the Muslim was brought to the hospital by the police to face the father of the child, he was very frightened. The father said, "I am a Christian, and we are taught to forgive, so I forgive you." Later that Muslim became a Christian. There is another true story about a young Muslim girl who attended a secondary school a few years ago and made friends with a popular Armenian girl, Annette. After one class, when Annette was not there, the teacher made an announcement that the children were to make sure they washed their hands if they ever shook hands with Annette – because she was a Christian, she was *Najiz*, unclean. Her young Muslim friend could not accept that Annette was unclean, and this then made her wonder about Annette's Christian religion. A few years later, that Muslim girl, and eventually over thirty members of her family, became Christian.

The Anglican and Presbyterian churches which were established in the late nineteenth century have also been a faithful witness in Iran. The Anglicans and the Presbyterians were backed by UK and US missions respectively and so have been attacked by the present regime as being the tools of imperialism. This, though, was not the experience of ordinary Iranians. In the tradition of nineteenth-century mission, they established schools and hospitals which helped thousands of people and won universal respect. So, for example, the head of the Anglican hospital in Shiraz was awarded the freedom of the city after many years of service.

The most recent overground church to be founded in Iran grew out of an indigenous charismatic prayer meeting in the late 1950s, and later developed into a church, taking the Assemblies of God name. This church has been very active in evangelism. At great risk to their own lives they have shared the gospel with many since the revolution. One member of this church alone gave away thousands of copies of the *Jesus* film, based on Luke's Gospel. Only two people refused to take a copy, showing that people have appreciated the gift.

Many Iranians might not have heard about these churches, but they will probably know about their martyrs. As devotees of Hussein, Iranians have an instinctive respect for those willing to die for their cause. So they will respect both these Christians who have paid the ultimate price for Christ, and the church they come from. And, seeing the continued courage of Christians as they distribute New

Testaments and hold meetings despite the threat of prison or worse also increases their respect for Christians, and makes them open to their faith.

Another factor about the church that has increased its standing among Muslims is the fact that whenever disaster has struck Iran, Iranian Christians have always been on the scene giving what help they can. They were there feeding the Kurds fleeing from Saddam after Operation Desert Storm (1990); and they helped the victims of recent earthquakes, including the devastating one in 2003 in Bam that killed 60,000 people in a few minutes. Whenever Christians have tried to stay, as they did in Bam to minister to children and orphans, the authorities have eventually stepped in to close down the work. But Iranians have noticed that Christians are people who are not frightened to get their hands dirty, and are more than willing to help out their fellow citizens.

A final area where the church has provided a faithful witness is in the conduct of its spiritual life. It is marked by joy and prayer.

In many Muslim gatherings there is a lot of grieving – indeed the heart of the Shi'a calendar is the death of Hussein at Karbala and this is mourned over very intensely. All Iranian Muslims will be familiar with the wailing and beating of chests that goes with this mourning. Thankfully, the Iranian Christians are very joyful in their faith, and when the Iranian

Muslim enters the meeting, they cannot help but notice this joy that flows from the believers. In their hearts they say, "We have spent so much time crying over Ali and Hussein, but look where we have got to – why don't we try this Jesus who gives his people so much joy?" This is the testimony of one Iranian lady about what she felt in the church: "In the church my spirit senses a wonderful presence of something. In that atmosphere I feel I am not alone . . ."

They will also notice the amount of time Iranian Christians give to prayer. Both the overground and the underground believers are people of prayer. There is prayer and fasting before many meetings, there is prayer during the meeting, and there is a lot of prayer after the meeting. Whole congregations will commit to pray and fast to see problems solved. And they see great answers, and they share these with their friends.

There was a boy who was very sick in a hospital. He was known to a lady in an underground church who had a great burden to go and pray for him, but the mother of the boy was very hostile to Christianity. She had reportedly said that she would prefer her boy to die rather than be prayed for in the name of Jesus Christ. The Christian lady persevered and decided to visit the boy – but she got the whole church praying. As she approached the boy's hospital bed, she saw the mother standing there and became so nervous that she just walked on and went up to the next bed. Here there was another family and she asked whether she could pray for the patient in the name of Jesus. They were delighted and commented on how kind it was for a complete stranger to give up her time to come and pray. While she prayed she noticed out of the corner of her eye that the mother of the sick boy had been watching the whole time.

When she had said her goodbyes to the other family, her nerves still got the better of her and she wasn't able to approach the mother. But the mother approached her. She said, "Can you pray for my son? The doctors have given him a few weeks to live."

The lady replied, "Yes, of course, but I will pray in the name of Jesus. Do you mind?"

"No, please pray in the name of Jesus," answered the mother.

So the Christian, whose whole church had been praying for this visit, laid hands on this sick boy in the name of Jesus. And a few weeks later he was completely well.

It is appropriate that prayer is the final factor as we consider why Iranians are so open despite the hostility of their government to Christianity. For, though cultural factors play a part, ultimately it is not a person's background that can bring them to faith in Jesus Christ, but only a divine revelation. And surely there is a link between prayer and revelation. In the past, thousands of prayers, with tears, have been offered to God for the Iranian people. And right now around the world there are thousands of intercessors asking God to send down a spirit of revelation on the people of Iran. And, as noted here, the Iranian church is a praying church.

It would seem God is answering this prayer in our generation.

The future

The underground church

The Iranian government, committed to the glory of Islam, seeking to hasten the return of Mahdi and deeply suspicious of the "Christian" West is actively strangling the established churches. The government is driving Christianity underground and here, in thousands of ordinary homes throughout the length and breadth of the country, a new church is growing that might one day emerge to change the whole character of the Middle East.

For this new underground church has three key characteristics that make continued vibrant growth very likely.

Firstly, and most importantly, is the very fact that this church is *underground*, i.e. hidden from the authorities. And it is likely to remain so as these believers are exceptionally cautious. Underground believers will rarely give their real names to each other, and certainly never to outsiders. They will change their meeting places frequently, and will not sing any worship songs if they have any doubts about their neighbors. This strict caution means it is difficult for the government to find out about them and this makes it much easier for sincere seekers to be drawn in. For if they walk into a church building it is obvious what they are doing; but if they are just going round to see a friend there is no need for others to know that they are in fact attending a Christian service. It is indeed humanly impossible for some people to attend a meeting in a church building; the risk to their career or even security is just too great. Now, though, with the underground churches, there are safer doors for seekers to knock on, and with much less risk of ever being found out.

The second characteristic that makes vibrant growth likely is the fact that the underground churches are very active. These Christians have absolutely no experience of church traditions, indeed 99 per cent of them will have never entered a church building, having come to faith through the media or personal evangelism. So as one of them said, "We just read the Bible and do what it says." One thing they understand, from the Scriptures and the witness in their own hearts, is that they must go out and tell others. But, also from reading the New Testament, especially Acts, they understand they have to be led by the Holy Spirit for their witnessing to be successful. So, before going out, the church will first spend up to two weeks in prayer and fasting. Then they will go wherever they believe the Holy Spirit is leading them.

Two ladies believed the Holy Spirit wanted them to distribute New Testaments on the inter-city buses. After much prayer and fasting they set out with their bags packed and got on one of these buses. Once the journey had begun the driver put on a video for people to watch – and to the amazement of these two ladies, the film he chose was *The Passion of the Christ*. This confirmed to them that they had indeed been led by the Holy Spirit.

After the film finished, the driver stopped for a break and everyone was milling outside the bus stretching their legs. The two ladies heard two young men talking about the film. One was asking whether it could be true that Jesus was crucified, and the other, clearly more skeptical, said of course not, and that what they had just seen was all Hollywood nonsense. His friend said it would still be good if they could read for themselves about Jesus, and how frustrating it was that you could not get Bibles easily in Iran.

At this point, one of the ladies could not keep quiet. She apologized for overhearing their conversation and then said, "I am a Christian. You can have my New Testament if you like." The first young man was overjoyed and could not believe she really meant it.

Then, rather shyly, the other young man who had been more skeptical said, "If I gave you my address, would you send one to me?"

"Well," replied the lady, "my friend is also a Christian and she might have a spare one."

In fact her friend had about sixteen in her bag! So both these young men received New Testaments.

The underground church is safer for seekers to attend; the church is actively looking for seekers, as the story above shows – and, finally, when the new comer is eventually allowed to attend a meeting (they are dealt with individually to begin with), they participate in a style of service which has been developed by the other Christians. And they, the new believer, will soon contribute to that style. This situation has two major advantages which make growth likely. First of all, it means the style of the meeting is likely to develop in a way that this particular social group enjoys. They will want to win people to Christ who are similar to themselves, and they will then come and also enjoy the milieu of the group. So the church will grow, because new Christians like to attend meetings where other people are like themselves. This is what church growth studies around the world have shown.[46] Overground churches inevitably tend to develop a style of service and organization that is more formal and less free to adapt, so not all members always feel comfortable.

The second great advantage of this situation which is likely to result in more growth is that the underground church member gains a sense of ownership in their church very quickly. While the informal setting lends itself to all being involved in the decision-making process, the security situation makes it an absolute necessity: as all can be endangered by a decision, so all must be involved. Again church growth studies have identified ownership as a key issue in determining how fast a church grows. Obviously there are disadvantages with this situation as there is the possibility of extreme teaching or odd worship styles being introduced by strong personalities. However, in other situations around the world, most notably China and earlier in Soviet Russia, the advantages that lead to growth outlined here far outweigh these dangers. Also with modern communication these groups are not entirely isolated from the international church and can receive pastoral advice.

These three characteristics, then, mark the underground church in Iran: it is hidden from the authorities; it is active; and its style and organization is wholly owned by its members. The immediate future of Christianity in Iran rests with this church. Given the openness of the Iranian people, and these characteristics, it is reasonable to conclude that the future of Christianity in Iran is truly exciting.

Role of international church

The church in Iran will grow because of the ministry of faithful Christians inside the country. However, there is still much the international church can do. Millions of Iranians now have satellite TV and many are watching Christian programs and people are phoning in to receive Christ. Also millions of Iranians either have the internet in their homes, or they regularly visit internet cafés, of which there are thousands, where they can access hundreds of Christian websites. All of this new media, which is playing such a crucial role, is being operated outside Iran and needs the support of the international church. As we have already learned, all the printing of Scriptures and Christian literature in Persian is strictly illegal, so this must happen outside Iran and then be taken in for believers. Again, the role of the international church in this area is crucial.

There is also the fact that an estimated four million Iranians now live outside Iran. They have also proved to be very open to Christianity and there are now Persian-speaking Christian fellowships in New Zealand, Australia, Japan, Thailand, India, Pakistan,

Ukraine, Turkey, Greece, Austria, Germany, France, Holland, Finland, Sweden, Denmark, Belgium, Holland, UK, the USA, Canada and quite possibly other countries as well. The fact that many more Iranian Muslims in the Diaspora have turned to Christ than for example Pakistanis or Malaysians underlines the whole argument of this book. It also highlights the importance of the international church, for if Christians in these host countries had not reached out with the gospel to Iranians, these fellowships would not now exist. So it is very important that the international church is aware of how open Iranians in their midst are and reach out to them. This will not only dramatically change the lives of the Iranians, but also this will impact Iran as there is constant contact between Iranians in the Diaspora and the home country. When Iranians come to Christ abroad, they long to see their family members saved, and so the gospel is shared. Some will even return to Iran with the express purpose of sharing their faith with their extended family.[47] So outreach to Iranians by the international church can have a wide-reaching impact inside Iran.

Finally, there is the issue of advocacy, for when Iranian Christians are intimidated, unfairly imprisoned, or even put on trial for their lives they desperately need to know that their worldwide family cares and will speak out. In September 2004, an officer in the army was imprisoned for being an active Christian. When he was brought to trial the judge is reported to have said, "I don't know who you are, but apparently the rest of the world does. You must be an important person, because many people from the government have called me, saying to cancel your case."[48] This illustrates the importance of advocacy work, another key area where the international church can get involved in helping the church in Iran.

CONCLUSION

Iranian church history has entered a new and intriguing chapter. With hardliners Ayatollah Khamenei and President Ahmadinejad in power for the foreseeable future, the seeming outlook for the church could not be bleaker. These men, either for political or genuine religious reasons, are determined to see the glory of Islam throughout Iran, and create conditions that will hasten the return of the Twelfth Imam, Mahdi. This closes the land to the gospel, as does the regime's profound mistrust of both Western politics and values, which they see as being "Christian" and dangerous for the Muslim world.

Iran is a closed land, yet Iranians are very open to the gospel of Jesus Christ.

They have been deeply disillusioned with the war, economic chaos and totalitarianism that the Islamic Republic has brought them. This has made them question whether God is really behind the Islam preached by their government. And they are ready to question because their Iranian identity is not fully cemented into Islam. They are also very aware that their ancestors (Cyrus, Darius) led one of the world's greatest civilizations long before the arrival of Islam, and their poetry constantly reminds them that the language of their heart, Persian, is not the language of their religion, Arabic. Furthermore, their poetry takes them to an intellectual landscape that as well as being much more tolerant than the dogmas of the mosque, is also essentially ambivalent towards Islam. And many Iranians know their poetry a lot better than they do the holy books of their religion.

All of this makes Iranians more than ready to consider the claims of Jesus Christ. And when they do, they do not meet someone who is completely alien to their background. Indeed they recognize the characteristics of heroes they have always been taught to revere. In Jesus they see Ali's love for the poor, Hussein's willingness to be a sacrifice for others, and Mahdi, who though unseen is still present and who one day will return to judge the world. Possibly there is a suspicion and caution about Western Christianity amongst Iranians, but there is an instinctive attraction to the Man from Galilee. For he represents all they long to see in a hero. Once attracted to Jesus Christ, the prevalence of Sufism amongst Iranians means that the expectation for them to have an intuitive experience of him is already there. So when asked to sense the work of the Holy Spirit, or to ask Christ into their hearts, this is not wholly foreign to the Iranian. Until recently, the person sharing with them would usually have been a part of a church organization that had been originally started by foreigners; indeed, the Iranian might have feared that by becoming a Christian they were somehow being less than loyal to their national identity. Now, though, it is most likely that there is no such connection. The person sharing just belongs to a group of Iranian "believers". This too makes it a lot easier for the person who began by just considering Christ, to then become a fully committed Christian.

This argument does not want in any way to undermine the transforming power of the Holy Spirit, or the power of a stubborn soul committed to sinful rebellion. For however attracted an Iranian might be to Jesus, ultimately only the unique authority of the Holy Spirit can reveal the living Jesus Christ to them. And if they are determined to live in sin, all of their attraction and interest in experiencing God is worthless. However, individuals, families, social groups and indeed entire nations can pass through a period when certain factors come together whereby the gospel of Jesus Christ is that much more appealing. It is the argument of this short book that the Iranian people might well be beginning to pass through such a period in our generation.

The famous thirteenth-century Iranian poet, Mowlavi or Jalal al-Din Rumi, revered in his homeland, wrote a wonderful poem about how the lame and blind should come to Jesus ('Isa) for healing.

> The house of 'Isa was the banquet of men of heart
> O afflicted one, quit not this door.
> From all sides the people ever thronged
> Many blind and lame, halt and afflicted
> At the door of the house of 'Isa at dawn,
> That with his breath he might heal their ailments.[1]

We have learned that some in Iran fear Christianity and try to keep their land closed to the gospel; but we have also seen that there are many others who listen to their poet. Feeling afflicted by all that has happened in their country, they are going to the door of the house of Isa, wherever that might be, and as has always been true, he binds up the broken-hearted.

These broken-hearted soon share their story with other open hearts, and so the church of Jesus Christ is growing in Iran.

ENDNOTES

1. A CLOSED LAND

[1] See "Iran Hardliner Sweeps To Victory" http://news.bbc.co.uk/1/hi/world/middle_east/462 1249.stm *Angus Reid Global Monitor*, Iran, http://www.angus-reid.com/tracker/index.cfm?fuse-action=viewItem&itemID=5070.

[2] For a fuller discussion of this relationship see Sandra Mackay's *The Iranians* (London: Penguin, 1996), chapter 4, The Faces of Authority: Father, King, and Cleric.

[3] See Roy Muttahadeh's excellent *The Mantle Of The Prophet* (Oxford: Oneworld Publications, 1985), page 172 regarding the traditional view of government before Mahdi's return.

[4] Eileen Humphreys, *The Royal Road* (Essex, UK: Scorpion Publishing Ltd., 1991), page 237.

[5] For more on Reza Shah's confrontation with the clergy see Sandra Mackay's *The Iranians*, pages 181–182.

6 Of the many chapters and articles dealing with Khomeini's campaign to oust the Shah, some of the best are to be found in Baqer Moin's outstanding biography, *Khomeini, The Life Of The Ayatollah* (New York: Thomas Dunne Books, 1999) chapters 9,10 and11.

7 For Washington's reaction to the fall of the Shah, see Kenneth Pollack's *The Persian Puzzle* (London: Random House, 2005), pages 147–148.

8 For a very helpful diagram illustrating the nature of Iran's government, see "Who Runs Iran", www.bbc.co.uk.

9 Q & A Iranian Election Row, February 2004 by BBC's Jim Muir. http://news.bbc.co.uk/1/hi/world/middle_east/3452839.stm.

10 For a helpful discussion both of the *Komitehs* and the Revolutionary Guards, see Kenneth Pollack's *The Persian Puzzle*, pages 150–151.

11 *The Koran*, translated by N.J. Dawood (London: Penguin Books, 1956).

12 The original English translation was published by the International Islamic Federation of Students Organizations translated by Ezzeddin Ibrahim and Denys Johnson-Davies. Seehttp://www.islamworld.net/nawawi.html.

13 Translation of *Sahih Bukhari* by Muhammad Muhsin Khan, Section 84 http://www.usc.edu/dept/MSA/fundamentals/hadithsunnah/bukhari/

14 Address by President Ahmadinejad to UN, www.um.org.

15 For an excellent discussion on Mahdi, see Vali Nasr, *The Shia Revival* (New York: W.W. Norton & Company, 2006), pages 67–68.

16 Scott Peterson, "Waiting For The Rapture In Iran", December 2005, page 2, www.csmonitor.com.

17 See also the fascinating "Waiting for the Mahdi: Official Iranian Eschatology Outlined in Public Broadcasting Program in Iran", available at the Middle East Media Research Centre (MEMRI), www.memri.org.

18 See http://www.iranian.ws/cgi-bin/iran_news/exec/view.cgi/13/10945/printer.

19 See "The Frightening Truth Of Why Iran Wants A Bomb" by Amir Taheri, April 2006, www.telegraph.co.uk.

20 See "President Sees Light Surrounding Him" by Golnaz Esfandiari November 29 2005. http://www.iran-press-service.com/ips/articles-2005/november-2005/ahmadi_revelations_291105.shtml.

21 See "The Frightening Truth Of Why Iran Wants A Bomb" by Amir Taheri, April 2006, www.telegraph.co.uk.

22 Scott Peterson, "Waiting For The Rapture In Iran", December 2005, page 2, www.csmonitor.com.

23 See "The Rise of Prof Crocodile, A Hardliner To Terrify Hardliners" by Colin Freeman 19/11/2005, www.telegraph.co.uk.

24 See Payvand's *Iran News*, December 1 2001 http://www.netnative.com/news/01/jan/1072.html.

[25] See Mohammad Teghi Mesbah-Yazdi, www.brainyen-cyclopeida.com.

[26] See "The Rise of Prof Crocodile, A Hardliner To Terrify Hardliners" by Colin Freeman 19/11/2005, www.tele-graph.co.uk.

[27] See Mohammad Teghi Mesbah-Yazdi, www.brainyen-cyclopeida.com.

[28] www.mesbahyazdi.org.

[29] Colin Freeman, *Sunday Telegraph/Washington Times*, February 19 2006.

[30] "Clerics jockey for power as Iranian vote nears" by Nazila Fathi, *The New York Times*, September 25 2006, www.iht.com.

[31] Scott Peterson, "Waiting For The Rapture In Iran", December 2005, page 2, www.csmonitor.com.

[32] See Ramy Nima, *The Wrath of Allah* (London: Pluto Press, 1983), pages 5–6.

[33] For an excellent discussion on Mossadeq, see Kenneth Pollack's *The Persian Puzzle*, pages 52–71 or Sandra Mackay's *The Iranians*, chapter 7, "The Shah and The Prime Minister: Iran's Second Revolution".

[34] Sandra Mackay's *The Iranians*, page 207.

[35] "I know it is not popular for an American ever to say anything like this, but I think it's true [applause], and I apologized when President Khatami was elected. I pub-licly acknowledged that the United States had actively overthrown Mossadeq and I apologized for it . . ." *Executive Intelligence Review*, February 11 2005 issue.

Excerpts from President Clinton's interview with Charlie Rose.

36 See Eileen Humphreys, *The Royal Road*, page 241. For more detail, see Nikki Keddie's *Modern Iran* (New Haven and London: Yale University Press, 2003), page 137.

37 See Kenneth Pollack's *The Persian Puzzle*, page 74–77 for a fuller discussion regarding American military aid and SAVAK.

38 From the biography of Ayatollah Khamanei see http://www.islam-pure.de/imam/biograph/biogri-cel.htm.

39 This term had originally been used by Jalal Al-e Ahmad, a very popular writer in the 1960s. He warned Iranians of the danger of being cut off from their Shi'ite roots by chasing Western fashions.

40 See the Wise Sayings of and Guidelines by Imam Khomeini, Foreign Policy. http://www.irna.com/occa-sion/ertehal/english/saying/.

41 See http://english.aljazeera.net/English/archive/archive?ArchiveId=15816.

42 See "Iranian Drama TV Series", Dispatch 833, www.memri.org

43 See, "Protocols of The Elders Of Zion", www.ushmm.org.

44 So Ayatollah Khomeini, "America, this natural criminal that has set the world on fire and its colleague, world Zionism, to reach their objectives commit crimes that pens and tongues are ashamed to describe."

http://www.irna.com/occasion/ertehal/english/say-ing/.

[45] "The problem & discrimination that Assyrians of Iran face", www.betnahrain.org.

2. OPEN HEARTS

[1] See "Saddam's Green Light" by Robert Parry, www.consortiumnews.com. Here he quotes from President Carter's memoirs: "As fate would have it, the Iraqis chose the day of [Tabatabai's] scheduled arrival in Iran, September 22, to invade Iran and to bomb the Tehran airport. Typically, the Iranians accused me of planning and supporting the invasion."

[2] For an excellent discussion on Ayatollah Khomeini's role in starting the war see Efraim Karsh's *The Iran-Iraq War 1980–1988* (Oxford: Osprey, 2002), pages 12–15.

[3] http://www.irna.com/occasion/ertehal/english/say-ing/.

[4] See Kenneth Pollack's *The Persian Puzzle*, page 199.

[5] See Baqer Moin's Khomeini, *The Life Of The Ayatollah*, page 251.

[6] See http://islamic-fundamentalism.info/chVI.htm.

[7] Quoted in Efraim Karsh's *The Iran-Iraq War 1980–1988*, page 62.

[8] See Kenneth Pollack's *The Persian Puzzle*, page 198.

[9] See "Iran–Iraq War 1980–1988", http://www.globalse-curity.org/military/world/war/iran-iraq.htm.

10 See Kenneth Pollack's *The Persian Puzzle*, page 238.

11 See Baqer Moin's Khomeini, *The Life Of The Ayatollah*, page 207.

12 See "Ayatollah Sadeq Khalkhali", www.telegraph. co.uk, November 2003.

13 See "Ayatollah Sadeq Khalkhali, Judge At The Islamic Revolutionary Tribunal, On The Defendant's Right To Counsel", www.abfiran.org.

14 Obituary: "Ayatollah Sadeq Khalkhali Hardline cleric known as the 'Hanging Judge' of Iran", Adel Darwish, The Independent, November 29 2003.

15 See "Ayatollah Sadeq Khalkhali", www.telegraph. co.uk, November 2003.

16 Obituary: "Ayatollah Sadeq Khalkhali Hardline cleric known as the 'Hanging Judge' of Iran", Adel Darwish, *The Independent*, November 29 2003.

17 See Baqer Moin's Khomeini, *The Life Of The Ayatollah*, pages 208–209.

18 See Baqer Moin's Khomeini, *The Life Of The Ayatollah*, page 239.

19 See Baqer Moin's Khomeini, *The Life Of The Ayatollah*, page 240.

20 The official number was seventy-two, the same number allegedly killed with Ali at Karbala.

21 See Baqer Moin's Khomeini, *The Life Of The Ayatollah*, page 242.

22 Source: "The organ of the Islamic Student Societies, followers of the Mojahadin", no. 63, April 19 1982, page

14. A footnote in Ramy Nima's *The Wrath of Allah*, page 115.

[23] See Baqer Moin's Khomeini, *The Life Of The Ayatollah*, page 255, also Robin Wright's *In The Name Of God* (London: Bloomsbury, 1990), page 124.

[24] See Baqer Moin's Khomeini, *The Life Of The Ayatollah*, pages 278–279.

[25] See Sandra Mackay's *The Iranians*, pages 235–237.

[26] See "Lifestyle of Imam Khomeini", www.inminds. co.uk.

[27] See Baqer Moin's *Khomeini, The Life Of The Ayatollah*, page 258.

[28] For the revolution's immediate impact on the economy see Ramy Nima's *The Wrath of Allah*, pages 116–120; see also Helen Chapin Metz, ed. *Iran: A Country Study* (Washington: for the Library of Congress, 1987), "Role Of The Government" http://countrystudies.us/iran/63.htm; see also Sandra Mackay's *The Iranians*, pages 338–343.

[29] For more on the Iranian economy since the 1980s, see Elaine Sciolino's *Persian Mirrors* (New York: Free Press, 2000), pages 321–335, and Sandra Mackay's *The Iranians*, pages 360–361.

[30] For a fuller discussion about bonyads, see "Millionaire Mullahs", Paul Klebnikov, July 2003, www.forbes.com.

[31] Statement of Kenneth Katzman Specialist in Middle Eastern Affairs Congressional Research Service, July 25 2006, http://jec.senate.gov/Documents/ Hearings/ katzmantestimony.

[32] See Elaine Sciolino's *Persian Mirrors*, pages 328–329.

[33] See Elaine Sciolino's *Persian Mirrors*, page 317.

[34] There is a great Iranian film, *Offside* by Jafar Pahani with this frustration as the main storyline.

[35] See *Reporters Sans Frontiers* – Iran, February 2003, www.rsf.org/article.php3?id_article=12636.

[36] See Elaine Sciolino's *Persian Mirrors*, page 103.

[37] See "Iran: Girl With Mental Age of Eight Given Death Sentence After Mother Forced Her Into Prostitution From Early Age", http://www.amnesty.org.uk/news_details.asp?NewsID=15803.

[38] "Iran: Stoning for 'adultery' – a women's issue", www.wluml.org/english/.

[39] The homosexual magazine Outrage puts the number at 4,000, see "Iran – The State-Sponsored Torture & Murder of Lesbians & Gay Men. New evidence of how the clerical regime frames, defames and hangs homosexuals" by Simon Forbes, April 2006, UK, http://www.peter-tatchell.net/international/iranstatemurder.htm.

[40] See "Iran: Death penalty/imminent execution: Karim Fahimi", http://web.amnesty.org/library/Index/ENGMDE130692005.

[41] *CIA World Fact Book*, https://www.cia.gov/library/publications/the-world-factbook/geos/ir.html.

[42] For an excellent discussion regarding the origins of Shi'ism and how it was adopted by Iran, see D. Donaldson, *The Shi'ite Religion* (London: Luzac, 1933) and the more recent *The Shia Revival* by Vali Nasr.

43 For wonderful descriptions of the re-enactment of Hussin's martyrdom in nineteenth-century Iran, see Roy Mottahedeh's *The Mantle Of The Prophet*, pages 173–179.

44 Many Iranians become Christians as a result of vivid dreams where they often meet Jesus as the "man in white".

45 See Samuel Moffett's *A History of Christianity in Asia*, Volume 1 (New York, Orbis Books, 1998), page 101.

46 For detailed and sustained study of the influence of this factor see Donald McGavern's classic *Understanding Church Growth* (Grand Rapids, MI: Eerdmans, 1980).

47 For example, an Iranian lady became a Christian through the Alpha Course in Sweden and went back to visit her parents in Iran. Christians were praying for her in Sweden and were very excited when she came back with the news that thirty-two of her extended families had accepted Christ.

48 On May 28 2005, a court in Bushehr acquitted Hamid Pourmand on further charges of apostasy and proselytizing. http://web.amnesty.org/library/index/eng-mde130602005.

CONCLUSION

1 See *Christ and Christianity in Persian Poetry* by H.B. Dehqani-Tafti (Cirencester: Sohrab Books, 1986), page 6. Bishop Dehqani, an expert on this subject, here quotes Rumi's poem from a translation by E.H. Whinfield.

FURTHER READING

Ahmadi, N and F., *Iranian Islam* (London: Macmillan Press, 1998)

Alavi, N., *We Are Iran* (London: Portobello Books, 2006)

Donaldson, D., *The Shi'ite Religion* (London: Luzac, 1933)

Edabi, S., *Iran Awakening* (London: Rider, 2006)

Foltz, R., *Spirituality In The Land Of The Noble* (Oxford: Oneworld Publications, 2004)

Hiro, D., *Iran Today* (London: Methuen, 2006)

Humphreys, E., *The Royal Road* (Essex, UK: Scorpion Publishing Ltd., 1992)

Karsh, E., *The Iran-Iraq War 1980–1988* (Oxford: Osprey Publishing, 2002)

Keddie, R., *Modern Iran* (New Haven and London: Yale University Press, 2003)

Mackay S., *The Iranians* (London: Penguin, 1996)

Moffat, S., *History of Christianity in Asia*, Volume 1 (New York: Orbis Books, 1998)

Moin, B., *Khomeini, The Life Of The Ayatollah* (New York: Thomas Dunne Books, 1999)

Mottahedeh, R., *The Mantle Of The Prophet* (Oxford: Oneworld Publications, 1985)

Nasr, V., *The Shia Revival* (New York: W.W. Norton & Company, 2006)

Nima, R., *The Wrath of Allah* (London: Pluto Press Ltd., 1983)

Pollack, K., *The Persian Puzzle* (London: Random House, 2004)

Sciolino E., *Persian Mirrors* (New York: Free Press, 1997)

Waterfield, R., *Christians In Persia* (Sydney: Allen and Unwin, 1973)

Wright, R., *In The Name Of God* (London: Bloomsbury, 1990)